ELIZABETH BEACON

Secrets of the Viscount's Bride

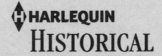

HARLEQUIN®
HISTORICAL™

Recycling programs for this product may not exist in your area.

ISBN-13: 978-1-335-72379-6

Secrets of the Viscount's Bride

Copyright © 2023 by Elizabeth Beacon

For questions and comments about the quality of this book, please contact us at CustomerService@Harlequin.com.

Harlequin Enterprises ULC
22 Adelaide St. West, 41st Floor
Toronto, Ontario M5H 4E3, Canada
www.Harlequin.com

Printed in U.S.A.

Elizabeth Beacon has a passion for history and storytelling and, with the English West Country on her doorstep, never lacks a glorious setting for her books. Elizabeth tried horticulture, higher education as a mature student, briefly taught English and worked in an office before finally turning her daydreams about dashing piratical heroes and their stubborn and independent heroines into her dream job: writing Regency romances for Harlequin Historical.

Books by Elizabeth Beacon

Harlequin Historical

Falling for the Scandalous Lady
Lady Helena's Secret Husband
Secrets of the Viscount's Bride

The Yelverton Marriages

Marrying for Love or Money?
Unsuitable Bride for a Viscount
The Governess's Secret Longing

The Alstone Family

A Less Than Perfect Lady
Rebellious Rake, Innocent Governess
One Final Season
A Most Unladylike Adventure
A Wedding for the Scandalous Heiress

Visit the Author Profile page
at Harlequin.com for more titles.

Prologue

'**Y**ou will do this for us, won't you, Martha? Please say you will!' Lady Fetherall begged with tears in her eyes.

'I'm a hill farmer, Caro, not an actress. We live such different lives. How could I fool anyone into thinking I am you for a whole week? I doubt I could manage it for half an hour,' Martha protested.

'You were such a clever mimic when we were little. I don't remember much about the time before Papa died, but I know you used to imitate people to make me laugh and you were always getting in trouble for it.'

'That was a childish game, and anyway, isn't it a crime to impersonate someone with the intent to deceive?'

'I don't know, but since you wouldn't be deceiving me, then probably not.'

'I'd be deceiving your viscount, though, wouldn't I?'

'Stop saying that,' her half-sister said with a shudder that gave away her feelings towards the man she was supposed to marry in two weeks' time. 'He's not *my* viscount. Even if I had never met Richard and fallen in love with him, Lord Elderwood would only be a stiff and chilly aristocrat to me.'

'He'd be *your* stiff and chilly aristocrat if Mr Harmsley hadn't persuaded you to marry him instead, though, wouldn't he?'

'True,' Caro said with a grimace and a look of such blank horror that Martha began to wonder if this viscount her sister was engaged to was just a more important version of Caro's repellent first husband. *She* shuddered at the thought of a repeat of that awful and sometimes violent marriage for her sister, so she hated to think how Caro felt. 'There's something else I must tell you, Martha,' Caro confessed but avoided Martha's questioning gaze.

She felt a rush of affection for the half-sister she saw so seldomly, thanks to their heartless and manipulative grandfather, Alderman Tolbourne. She recalled Caro looking the other way and wringing her hands just like this when they were small children, before their grandfather had parted them. He had done it on the pretext that Martha was a disgrace to the family name because she was born with red hair and there was none of it in his family or her lying dam's either—or so he said. Therefore she could not be his son's child but must be another man's bastard imposed on Sam Tolbourne by the designing harpy who lured him into running away with her when he was barely out of the schoolroom.

Martha knew her father and mother must have truly loved one another to do such a thing, and that they had had to elope once her mama realised she was with child. Tolbourne had had such grand plans for his only child, and he had forbidden her mother and father from having anything more to do with one another. She had been old enough to hear that story from her father before he died, but Caro hardly remembered him now. How utterly lonely her half-sister must have been when their grandfather filled her young ears with a distorted version of their impulsive but loving papa and took from her even the memories of his warmth and affection for both his daughters.

'Best get it over with, then, Caro,' she said gently.

'I am with child, Marty,' Caro said in a rush, as if that was the only way she could say it without bursting into overwrought tears.

'Goodness…' she said lamely. It felt so odd to think of her vulnerable half-sister being a mother in a few months. Caro had been married to the dreadful Sir Ambrose Fetherall for years until he fell downstairs while drunk and broke his neck. It must have been such a relief *that* union had proved to be fruitless, but what a shock to find she was increasing and wasn't married to the child's father.

'Did you know about the baby when you became engaged to Viscount Elderwood?' she said.

'Yes, but Grandfather gave me no choice but to agree to his proposal and I dare not tell Lord Elderwood I don't want to marry him. Even without the baby I wouldn't marry him, Caro. Titles mean nothing to me, and I just want to be loved and Richard really does love me.'

Well, obviously he says he does since he's got you with child, Martha's inner cynic whispered, but she told it to be quiet. What a mess, even if it was Charlton Tolbourne's fault for forcing Caro into this marriage of inconvenience. It felt like Martha's duty to at least try to stop Caro being forced to marry one man with another one's child in her belly. She would have to do this, then. It was the only way Caro and her lover could marry without their grandfather finding out and forcing Caro into another marriage against her will. It looked like a pitifully poor chance, since it depended on Martha acting the fine lady for days at a time, but it was one they would have to take.

'I suppose it is Mr Harmsley's baby and not your viscount's?'

'Of course it is,' Caro said indignantly. 'I love Richard. I couldn't let another man touch me like that now. And will you please stop calling him *my* viscount.'

'You are engaged to him and I had to ask.'

'I suppose so.'

'How do you feel about the baby?' Martha asked warily.

'Scared,' Caro said and she looked it. She seemed to search for words to explain, 'yet so very happy it will be Richard's child so I can love it and him.'

Martha understood. Even gentle Caro would have found it very hard to love Fetherall's child. Martha felt the old weight of trying to make her little half-sister's life as their late father would have wanted it; she certainly hadn't been very successful since his death. Caro deserved to be happy after a lonely childhood and unhappy first marriage, but Martha couldn't help but feel a painful pang of jealousy because her half-sister was about to experience the joy she had longed for so desperately herself when her dear Tom Lington was alive. She still had an aching void in her heart and Tom had gone to his watery grave five years ago at the Battle of Trafalgar. If he were alive, he would tell her to open her heart to her half-sister and the family Harmsley and Caro would have together. So, it looked as if this mad scheme to take her half-sister's place while Caro and Harmsley raced to Scotland to marry by declaration was a wild risk she must take. Besides, she would have Noakes, her sister's devoted lady's maid, by her side to help her with the deception.

'I am terrified Grandfather will force me to wed this man, even if he finds out I am with child, Martha.'

'But you are not a seventeen-year-old girl to be forced up the aisle against your will this time, Caro. You are a widow of three and twenty and legally entitled to marry whomever you choose.'

'Try telling Grandfather that. He has had me watched ever since he found out that I was meeting Richard in secret. That's why I had to ask you to come here to meet me instead of at Noakes's sister's house in Islington as usual. Even Grandfather's thugs can hardly push their way into an exclusive London modiste's premises when I am supposed to be choosing my trousseau. You know better than anyone how ruthless Grandfather can be, given what he did to you. We wouldn't be so alike if there was an ounce of truth in that wicked story he set about when we were little.'

Martha shuddered. 'I see what you mean.'

'Nothing matters to him except getting his own way and he wants his great-grandson to be a lord one day. He claims Papa let him down by marrying first one doxy then another—and they were our mothers for heaven's sake, Martha, even if we don't remember them.'

'We know they were good women and Papa loved them because he was a good man and not a bit like his father. But you're quite right about Tolbourne. I was only six when he threw me out and he must have known it was a lie even as he accused me of being a bastard and not Papa's child at all.'

'If only I hadn't hidden behind you and been so shy I wouldn't even speak to anyone else, he might have let us grow up together,' Caro said with a helpless shrug.

'Don't you dare blame yourself, Caro. He did it because I defied him. Papa said I must protect my little sister if ever he wasn't able to, and Tolbourne was so cold and stern that you were terrified of him. You were so little; it was all his fault and never yours. He must have decided to turn you into a lovely husband hunter from the day he first saw us and realised

I would fight his plans every step of the way if he kept me. I admit I was surprised when he made you marry a mere baronet the first time.'

'Grandfather couldn't buy his way into the *ton* proper for a titled husband back then so he made do with Brose. Brose's title got me into the fringes of it, despite his shocking reputation. But Grandfather is richer now thanks to his shady dealings during this horrid war, so he can afford the lord he always wanted me to marry this time.'

'Why not tell Lord Elderwood you are with child, Caro? Lords are always desperate for an heir, and the prospect of a cuckoo in his nest is sure to horrify him.'

'Grandfather must have some sort of stranglehold on him to force him to offer for me. What if I tell him and he decides to marry me anyway and tell the world my baby was stillborn so it could be put in an orphan asylum?'

Martha felt a cold hand close on her heart at the thought of Caro's child left to fend for itself as she so nearly was herself as a child. But this was no time to recall old terrors when she had Caro and her baby to worry about. 'Why would he, Caro? That story sounds very far-fetched, even to me,' she said and hoped she was right.

'But what if I'm right?'

'Even if you are, Tolbourne can't force you up the aisle to wed this Lord Elderwood.'

'You think not? You don't know him as well as I do, then,' Caro said starkly.

'Thank goodness,' Martha said. 'But are you sure you can't confide in Lord Elderwood and save all this trouble?'

'No. He's set on marrying me, and I know I am only a means to an end. He thinks I don't matter enough to know what that end is, of course,' Caro said bitterly.

As Martha's younger sister wasn't usually bitter, despite so many reasons why she could be, the man must have treated her very coldly indeed. Martha decided she might as well hate him in addition to Tolbourne, and she had only been grasping at straws before, looking for an easier way out of this mess than the charade Caro was asking her to perform while she made a dash for Scotland with her lover.

'Oh, very well. If there's no other way to get you and Mr Harmsley safely wed without Tolbourne and his tame viscount finding out, then I suppose I will have to do it,' she finally conceded.

'Oh, thank you, Martha. You have always been a better sister to me than I deserve,' Caro said, seeming on the verge of overwrought tears before she blinked them back. 'But we don't have much time and you need to learn much about me and about Grandfather if you are going to convince people that you are me for long. It's as well, Grandfather thinks we haven't seen each other since the day he sent you away so it won't even occur to him we could have swapped places. I am so grateful to you; all three of us are.' Caro put a protective hand on her still flat stomach and met Martha's gaze with so much emotion in her dark eyes, which were so much like Martha's own.

However alike they looked—if you ignored the difference in hair colour—Martha had never had an unborn child to fight for. 'It's what sisters do,' she said. 'But how can you spend so much time with me if Tolbourne is having you watched so closely?'

'Celine is Noakes's niece and she's really called Sally, by the way. She says you can stay here in her private apartment while I pretend I am being fitted for my trousseau, but really Noakes and I will be doing our best to turn you into a fine lady.'

'Good luck with that unlikely transformation, but for now I had better write to Grandmama Winton and tell her I have decided to visit a couple of my fellow naval widows while I am in the south and not to expect me home until Candlemas. I do hope it doesn't snow too hard before the beginning of February, Caro.'

Martha tried to think of all the gaps in the story so nobody would come looking for her and destroy their web of lies because she did have a real life to go back to. She could hardly expect Caro to know how vital it was to get food and water to even the hardy sheep that Martha and her maternal grandparents kept on their Cumberland hill farms when the snow came.

'I can pay for extra help if you like, just in case it does.'

'No, if Tolbourne found out and put two and two together it would sink us.'

'What a horrid thought,' Caro said with a shudder. 'But you won't leave Kent before the day of my supposed wedding to Lord Elderwood, even if you hear of blizzards in the north, will you, Martha? Richard and I need a week's head start to be sure of getting to Scotland fast enough to outwit them all at this time of year.'

'I promise to do everything I can to fool your viscount that I am embarrassingly eager to marry him. From the time he arrives at Tolbourne's country house until the day before the wedding—I do draw the line at leaving him waiting at the altar while I make a hasty getaway on the day itself.'

'Of course. Now, let's get on with your lessons in being me before you change your mind.'

Chapter One

Seven days later, Martha felt so stifled by her grandfather's overheated country house that she longed for the fresh air of her Cumberland home. Not that she could take much in, with Caro's corset pinching and confining her into a shape she hadn't known her body could endure until now. Outwardly she *was* the silk-clad mantrap their grandfather had made Caro become, but inside she was still Martha and longed to go home and resume the quiet, isolated country life she had enjoyed before this charade had begun.

She reminded herself how ruthlessly her grandfather had made Caro flaunt her fine figure and lovely face to catch a nobleman and she laughed to think she might actually owe him something for rejecting her so harshly and publicly as a child. At least hating him would lend her the courage to go downstairs and begin this pretence in earnest. She sighed at the memory of Caro arriving at Celine's exclusive West End establishment this morning, as arranged, supposedly to pick up her wedding gown. Instead of Caro returning home afterwards with the gown, Martha had come here in Caro's place. Meanwhile Caro had slipped out of the back door dressed as one of the seamstresses to meet her lover, who had been waiting impatiently for her a few streets away, to begin their escape.

Even knowing that she was her sister's only chance to escape, Martha guiltily longed to tear off her sister's showy gown, put on one of her own warm and practical ones and walk to the nearest posting house so she could catch the stagecoach to anywhere else but here. She also knew she couldn't do it to Caro. She had to stay here and pretend to be her sister for as long as she could get away with it to give them the best chance of success. It was only a week after all. Just one week until Caro's supposed wedding to Lord Elderwood.

Martha had spent days learning to dress and walk and talk like Caroline, Lady Fetherall, until she felt almost a stranger to herself. Now she simply had to *be* Caro until it was too late for their grandfather to drag her sister back to marry his tame viscount. She sent up a prayer for good weather for them all the way to the Scottish border; if it rained and the roads were a sea of mud, then the carriage would be slowed down while Tolbourne's good horses could be ridden hard across country if needs be. She could not afford to slip up—if anyone but Noakes, Caro's devoted maid, guessed that she was not Lady Fetherall… Martha couldn't bear to think about what might happen to her beloved sister and her baby.

You should be careful what you wish for, Martha Lington, Martha told herself sharply, because she needed a distraction from the unpleasant picture of Caro and Harmsley racing for the border with their grandfather and his thugs in relentless pursuit. Despite her urge to hide away at Greygil with her maternal grandparents after Tom's death, sometimes she had secretly longed to dress in fine clothes and feel truly feminine again, as Tom had liked to see her during his brief, precious periods of shore leave. But now she was used to the rough clothes she wore nearly all of the time because anything better would soon get ruined when she was helping to run Grandfather Winton's farms. She felt uncomfortable in Caro's outrageous gowns and this horrid corset, especially the gown of deepest crimson silk she was currently wearing. So much of her was on display that any man who wanted to could ogle her pushed-up breasts and the entirety of her shape under this flimsy excuse for a gown that clung to her newly voluptuous figure as if it loved her.

Dressed like this, she was going to have to pretend to be a sophisticated lady of fashion while His chilly Lordship—who Caro swore despised her—kept his guilty secrets. But she would win this game, and Lord Elderwood wouldn't even know he was playing it. She had been pampered and primped and painted until she hardly recognised herself. Her hair had been dyed to match Caro's dark brown locks, and

the last traces of Mrs Martha Lington were gone…
She took another look in the mirror and shook her
artfully tousled head at the very idea that she could
get away with this outrageous deception for even
one night. If he could see her now, whatever would
her beloved Tom make of her flaunting herself like
this? she wondered. She hastily blinked back tears
as she didn't want to have to spend another second
with those horrid eyelash curlers and the lampblack
to make sure her lashes matched Caro's again.

'You'll ruin the style,' Noakes rebuked her when
Martha pushed at the wild tumble of curls her sister's
lady's maid had so carefully arranged.

Martha stopped nervously twisting a dyed curl
around her finger and raised an artfully darkened
eyebrow at Noakes. 'This isn't a style, it's a mess,'
she said, 'but it's not your fault.' Martha tweaked the
low neckline of her sister's gown to see if there was
a sliver more modesty in it but there wasn't.

'Are you ready?' Noakes asked dubiously.

'No, but I'm going to do it anyway,' Martha said
with a last glance at the stranger in the mirror. All
she had to do now was go downstairs and become
publicly engaged to Lord Elderwood to keep the
hounds off her sister's scent. 'Thank you for all your
help with this and with getting my sister well on her
way to Scotland,' she said impulsively. 'I'm sure Tolbourne's men didn't suspect anything when I left
Celine's dressed in Caro's clothes, although I admit
that my heart was racing all the way here.'

'Mine was as well, but you've done well so far, Miss Martha.'

'Don't call me that here, Noakes—and in any case, I'm most definitely not a miss.'

'Just as well, dressed like that,' Noakes said brusquely and Martha grimaced. Lady Fetherall couldn't be late for her own engagement ball, so it was time to go downstairs and face it.

Zachary Chilton, Viscount Elderwood, waited at the bottom of the stairs for the woman he was going to marry, despite every instinct screaming *No*. He was a Chilton so his word was his bond, but right now such promises felt like the work of the devil. He had made them to his late father and grandmother so now he must marry a shop-soiled lady who was rumoured to have a parade of lovers. But Zach had promised his father and grandmother that he would get Holdfast Castle back in the family one day; it had felt like his duty to reclaim the lands and property his grandfather had gambled away, so here he was.

Duty was the very devil but he'd never thought it would feel this bitter to pay the price for his promise. If only Lady Fetherall had refused Zach's proposal, her grandfather wouldn't have been able to hold the promise of Holdfast as her dowry over him until their wedding made it real, and maybe the old man would have sold it to him instead. If only she had said no. he could have known he had tried everything he could to get the place back and even those reproachful ghosts could not blame him for getting on with the life he really wanted to live. Then he could hope to meet a woman he could love one day and marry her instead.

His father and mother had loved one another so deeply that his mother still mourned his father fifteen years on. He had wanted to experience a love like that himself, but now he never would. He was going to marry Lady Fetherall for Holdfast Castle instead. In a week's time. This was his duty. A Chilton had lost the once splendid DeMayne inheritance—well, not lost it, *gambled it away*—so it was his task as his late and unlamented grandfather's heir to get it back.

His grandmother had been born Lady Margaret DeMayne and had been the last of her line so she had been considered a fabulous catch when Zach's charming rogue of a grandfather married her. For generations, the DeMaynes had held Holdfast Castle for the King, before Scotland and England were united by the Scottish Crown and there were no more excuses for fighting. The DeMaynes had had to settle for being powerful Northumbrian earls. But Lady Margaret had married a wastrel for love, and her husband, the last Viscount Elderwood but one, had thrown her great heritage away on the turn of a card before shooting himself and avoiding the consequences. Zach's very young father and grandmother had had to work hard to get Flaxonby Hall and the Chilton estates out of debt. His father had died tragically young, so now it was Zach's duty, as promised, to regain the castle and lands his grandfather had lost. At last Holdfast was within his reach, even if the price he had been forced to pay for it meant losing his freedom and his integrity along with it.

Marriage to Lady Fetherall was the only way he could get Holdfast back so he would marry her. Zach had tried to persuade Tolbourne to sell him the now ramshackle castle and rundown estate often enough and had been refused. In a malicious twist of fate, Sir Ambrose Fetherall had died in a drunken fall at some gaming hell and Tolbourne had named his price for the Holdfast Estate: marriage to Tolbourne's granddaughter or the castle could crumble to the ground for all Tolbourne cared.

Zach had wondered whether he would be able to wait the old man out—and buy the estate at a knockdown price since it was worth barely anything nowadays—but Tolbourne was too cunning for that. He threatened to put an entail on the place so that only his granddaughter's children could ever own it, and Zach would never get his hands on it. Thus, either Zach had to wed a woman who dressed and behaved like an expensive courtesan, or let all hope of getting Holdfast back go forever, and he couldn't bring himself to do that. That was why he was standing at the foot of Tolbourne's vulgarly gilded stairs in this vulgarly gilded house, waiting for Lady Fetherall to come down, so their engagement could be celebrated in style and the countdown to this devil's bargain would begin.

It was his fault they were standing in Tolbourne's house at all, since he refused to drag his family into this sordid business or let Tolbourne puff himself up at Flaxonby Hall and try to force himself on Zach's neighbours. Every instinct he had was screaming *Run* but he made himself stand still until he felt like he could be carved from a block of marble. He had put the Chilton emerald on Her Ladyship's slender finger before Christmas and the announcement had gone out in the morning papers, so there was no going back now. He was here to marry the confounded woman, so marry her he must.

Marble turned to ice as Lady Fetherall made him wait like a supplicant at court or an enslaved Barbarian chief making a Roman holiday. Tolbourne had been proved right: every man did have his price and Zach was paying his. As he fumed silently and waited on Her Ladyship's finest triumph, inside he swore he would find a way to escape Tolbourne's clutches. He made himself take a deep breath and unclenched his fists, pretending he was indifferent to Tolbourne's gloating look.

At least he could make sure Tolbourne would never have this noble great-grandson he was already boasting about to his cronies. Zach had no desire to bed the woman, and once he had said his vows to her and got the deeds of Holdfast in his hand, he could walk away from the marriage. Zach's younger brother, Max, could carry on the family line if needs be, because Zach would not breed with such a dam as though he were a fine bit of bloodstock that Tolbourne had bought to improve his stables. Yes, that was an excellent idea, now he only had to get this week over with so he could ride away from Tolbourne and his flighty granddaughter at the end of it, knowing Holdfast was back in the family at last.

At last he heard the sound of light footsteps on the stairs and the rustle of Lady Fetherall's silk skirts. The expensive rustle of them sounded shockingly loud in the sudden silence as all eyes fixed on her instead of on him for once. Zach steeled himself to meet her rather blank dark gaze once again. If he concentrated on keeping his expression equally blank and his body still, he might not care that Lady Fetherall was gliding downstairs as if she hadn't a care in the world. She always dressed outrageously so he should not be shocked by her latest daring silk gown, but he still was. There was more of her on show than most women would be willing to reveal *en dishabille*, but Zach told himself he was immune to her lovely face and lush feminine figure so what did that matter? He was a mature male with all the usual inconvenient masculine needs so no wonder his body wanted to respond to a lush feminine figure displayed for any fool to gawp at. His body could want her but he would maintain a frosty distance, he told himself sternly. He preferred subtle allure and, as she sauntered towards him as if she had nothing to be ashamed of, Lady Fetherall certainly wasn't being subtle about hers.

Yet he still had to beat his ridiculous masculine response to her curvaceous feminine figure into submission. Her dark hair was teased into artful disarray, and her come-to-bed dark eyes held more of a challenge than they ever had before. It took everything he had to turn himself into ice again. He saw that a challenge in the bold look she threw at him like a weapon and, against his will, she intrigued him. He had never felt even fleeting curiosity about the woman behind the painted smile before so whatever was the matter with him?

A shiver of unease ran through him as he gazed back at her. He wished he had a quizzing glass to get a better look at her, but it was too late to pretend that even without one he couldn't see every last inch of bare skin she was flaunting in that outrageous gown. He thought he saw shock and defiance in her eyes but Tolbourne seemed quite happy with her sugar-sweet smile. Zach thought there was a fiercer light in her dark eyes than usual, and tonight her smile almost had a she-wolf's snarl hidden in it.

Why had he never tried to gauge the woman's true feelings about him and this wretched marriage before now? he wondered.

Because he was too furious at being trapped himself, he decided. Didn't she realise a husband forced into marriage would be impossible to live with? Not that he planned to actually live with her so he supposed it probably didn't matter if she did or not. He supposed she had managed to live with Fetherall for years so living with him would be child's play. Yet there was still something a lot more complicated than he had expected to see in her dark eyes as she met his full-on for the first time. He had previously thought her shallow as a summer puddle, but he found he was questioning that impression tonight. Had it been a case of ignorance being bliss? Or had he not given *her* feelings a second thought because he'd been wrapped up in his own misery and had no intention of consummating the marriage in any case?

'Lady Fetherall.' He greeted her stiffly to distract himself from a ridiculous fantasy of her rich curves exposed in the privacy of his bedroom at Flaxonby Hall for a very personal inspection that was never going to happen.

'Lord Elderwood?' she said with a clever hint of doubt in her husky voice, which was no doubt done with the purpose of making him look directly at her again.

He wondered what colour her dark eyes were by daylight and why he had never cared enough to think about them until now. No matter if they were mud coloured or as darkly enchanting as a goddess's, he wasn't going to stare into them for long enough to find out. If she were as faithless as rumour suggested, then the instant she took a lover he could sue the fool for criminal conversation with his wife and divorce her. He would keep the castle and there would be nothing Tolbourne could do about it.

It was the perfect plan, so he couldn't afford to admire her for turning up to their betrothal ball dressed in deepest scarlet like a flag of defiance.

'Shall we join the company, my lady?' he suggested, before Tolbourne could assert his authority in this vulgar excuse for a home and speak for him.

'Of course, my lord,' she replied with such masterly lack of enthusiasm that Zach was intrigued all over again.

She didn't sound on the brink of achieving a lifelong ambition of a viscountess's coronet. Perhaps she had a lover she wished she could marry instead, if only he had a title. Stiff with offended pride and an unexpected twinge of jealousy at the very idea of being less than her perfect would-be husband, Zach held out his crooked elbow to the woman he had come here to marry. He nearly jerked his arm away when she laid the tips of her fingers on his sleeve; it felt as if a bolt of lightning had shot clean through him.

It was a rush of revulsion; of course it was.

He hated her touch even through his dark evening coat and fine linen. This was distaste and not the most unwelcome jag of sensual curiosity he had ever experienced. *Liar*, his inner fool screamed, but he ignored it manfully.

'Get on with it,' Tolbourne rasped from behind them, and Zach glanced at Lady Fetherall to see how she felt about her grandfather's brusque order.

What a mistake that was. This close to her he could see far too much of her opulent bosom from his superior height. Her dark hair was piled up and teased into the usual artful disarray, and he wondered why he had never before felt such a strong temptation to run his fingers though it and make it even wilder? Her lips were just a little bit redder than they ought to be, but nevertheless were full and rich looking. The skilfully applied rouge on her cheeks and lampblack on her lashes caused a lady standing nearby to whisper in a manner that carried some distance, 'Lady Fetherall *paints*,' and of course she was quite right.

He realised that he didn't want her to show even more flesh if she curtseyed or exerted herself unduly on the dance floor. Fury at the idea of every sentient male here tonight gawping at her with lusty eyes threatened his steely front. If she were his sister, or cousin, or even his mistress, he would take exception to her manner of dress because no self-respecting woman would want to be this bold. He forced his gaze away from her tightly corseted figure and barely there gown and thought he saw another flash of fierce defiance in her sleepy-eyed gaze before she demurely lowered her eyelashes again.

He let his own gaze linger on her painted face and indecently exposed bosom to test the idea that she hated this fiasco as well, then ordered himself to be horrified that she would be his wife next week and his sudden suspicion a very different woman lived under the paint and show was wishful thinking. To prove it she sent him a witchy glance from under her darkened eyelashes to say she was very available for flirtation and maybe more if he was willing. His manhood agreed but Zach told it to behave itself again, and anyway, he was far more interested in the fierce spirit he had glimpsed under the showy front.

No, he had to be mistaken. She *must* be the empty-headed and lusty female everyone thought she was, or she would have put more trade in the silk merchants' direction and added an ell or so more of it to all her gowns. He could not understand why tonight she fascinated him when she was without a hint of mystery to tempt and intrigue and almost everything she had to offer was on show. He had never felt even a glimmer of attraction to her before, but now it threatened his certainty that he did not want to be here tonight and did not want to marry this woman. He reminded himself why he *was* here and what he really wanted from their ridiculous engagement as he led her into the dazzlingly lit and gaudy ballroom. When they got there, he held up his hand for silence before Tolbourne could do it for him.

'Ladies and gentlemen, I present to you my bride-to-be, Lady Fetherall,' he announced when the din abated. He held up their joined hands with the Chilton emerald sparkling so brightly on his betrothed's finger that it flashed green fire in the light of too many crystal chandeliers. No wonder it was so hot in here.

A suspicious shiver tried to run through him at the coldness of that green fire and the falseness of this hastily arranged marriage. His mother had always refused to wear the Chilton emerald. She said it was vulgar, old-fashioned and maybe even cursed. Since Zach didn't care about his affianced bride or whether the marriage was cursed, none of that had seemed to matter when he slipped it on her shaking finger. But now he recalled the avarice in Tolbourne's eyes the day this betrothal became official and shivered on her behalf. She had seemed oddly subdued about the famous old gem that looked so heavy on her slender finger. Now he felt her hand shake in his as one of Tolbourne's toadies began to clap and the rest took it up. She seemed to relax after an apprehensive glance at her grandfather, whose smug look must have reassured her all was well.

Why had Zach never realised how afraid of the ruthless rogue she was?

Because he hadn't cared enough to notice, he supposed. He shot her another sideways glance and corrected himself—she didn't look so much afraid as braced for a harsh rebuke.

Confound this feeling that there was far more to Lady Fetherall than he had ever let himself see before! It might even feel like his duty to defend her from the old man now that they were to be wed before the week was out. He knew this was Tolbourne's way of thumbing his nose at the *ton*—Zach had been born into it so his viscountess would be received into their midst whether they liked it or not.

He looked across at her and saw that Lady Fetherall seemed as pleased with herself as usual. Maybe she really was a painted doll, quite happy to go along with her grandfather's grandiose schemes in return for a life of luxury and as many sparse silk gowns as his money would buy her.

Of course there wasn't a fiery tempered and rebellious woman hiding under the surface. Though with so much creamy skin on display, Zach wished she was covered up for his own sake as well as hers.

Chapter Two

Tame? Why on earth did I think he was going to be anything of the sort? Martha had been so shocked by this fierce nobleman at her side she could hardly believe he was really supposed to have married her half-sister in a week's time.

Speaking for herself, she had forgotten that there was anyone else in the room when he glared up at her for the first time with those extraordinary ice blue eyes. She stepped down into the hall to meet his chilly gaze and very nearly betrayed herself by staring at him open-mouthed.

This viscount Caro was so desperate *not* to marry was tall and distinctive and vital…and quietly furious about the whole idea.

He made everyone else fade into the background and Martha looked past him to ensure this really was Lord Elderwood and not his friend or brother, but there was nobody else at the bottom of the stairs except for her grandfather. This fierce, icy, steely-eyed Viking really must be Lord Elderwood, then. He had glanced indifferently at her then away, as if she were hardly worth the effort of a second look. The thump of her heartbeat said it would have been so much easier for her to fool the entitled idiot she had been expecting to see instead of this man. She couldn't help but wonder how it would feel if she were the one who was supposed to be marrying him in a week's time…

Challenged, intimidated and secretly a little too excited at the idea of having a man like him as her lover, her inner rebel whispered, but she told it to go back to sleep and behave because that was never going to happen.

In another age she could easily imagine him at the head of a band of fierce Viking marauders intent on plunder. Her mouth went dry and her pulse raced, making it such an effort to walk calmly down the last few stairs as if he were any old nobleman when he very clearly was neither old nor ordinary looking.

How on earth had she thought she could deceive this powerful man for so long?

She had to try, of course, but it was going to take every ounce of willpower she had—and a good deal of luck besides—to keep this act up when she was with him.

Lord Elderwood was much younger than she had expected him to be, and with those streaks of pale gold sun bleached into his thick tawny locks he looked as honed and fierce as his Norse ancestors must have when they sailed the northern seas in search of plunder. She recalled that the Vikings had ruled parts of the north of England for many centuries; Caro had told her that his country seat was in Yorkshire, so maybe it was no wonder he looked much too fierce to take being trapped into this inconvenient marriage of Caro's lightly. For a moment she pitied him; it seemed wrong to see so much stern power brought low, but she must never forget that he was the enemy. His broad shoulders and narrow hips might set off his stark black evening coat to perfection, and though his spotless linen and plain grey silk waistcoat made him seem like the very picture of a civilised lord, the cool intelligence in his ice-cold eyes argued there was a warrior underneath it all.

She was surprised to see that right now he looked as if he would take any way out of this wretched ball-room he could find. At least they had something in common.

Lord Elderwood had already led her into the ball-room and made his curt announcement of their engagement, and she was annoyed to discover that she could not quite meet his hostile gaze again. She skipped to the braced sensitivity of his firm mouth instead. He would be a Viking warrior with the soul of a poet if his mouth was not set in such a hard line that the poetry couldn't get out. What a fanciful idea that was—he wasn't a poet or a Viking raider, and it would be shockingly disloyal of her if she listened to that sneaky inner voice whisper, *I would have chosen him and not Mr Harmsley, Caro.*

She glanced up at him and something hot and

needy threatened to pull her closer for a breathless moment. There was a question in his ice blue eyes now—a look that asked her, *Did that really just happen?* Then her heartbeat raced on and a rebellious part of her wanted to meet his challenge head-on and toss it back at him. She hadn't even dreamed of another man since Tom died, so how could she now? She shook her head and was brought down to earth by the feel of the unfamiliar long ringlets dancing against the bare skin of her shoulders. It reminded her that this was all a lie and she was really Tom Lington's busy widow, a hard-working woman who had nothing at all in common with an arrogant viscount.

'The guests are waiting for us to lead out the first dance, my lady,' he told her, as if she needed reminding. He dipped his head so slightly it was hardly even an apology for a bow.

'Are they indeed, Lord Elderwood?' she said, as if she hadn't noticed. She sank into a curtsey so low that it gave him an excellent view of her prominently displayed décolletage. She would force him to wonder how low a gown could be cut without her bosom spilling out of it altogether.

Take that blow to your chilly pride while your future wife flaunts herself as vulgarly as you expected her to, my lord, she silently challenged as she rose from her curtsey with the coyly inviting smile Caro and Noakes had spent so much time trying to get her to learn. It felt like the perfect weapon to use on him in this moment and, sure enough, his gaze went even icier than it had been before.

'You had best lead me into it, then, had you not, my lord?' she prompted him almost artlessly, trying to look as if she were blissfully unaware of how little he wanted to go through the formalities of their engagement ball. She heard a scud of heavy rain dash on the long windows as if even the elements were protesting at such a cynical betrothal. She felt a shiver slide down her spine as she gazed up at Lord Elderwood with a smile so false that it made her cheeks ache.

This is so very wrong; nothing good will come of it, that shiver argued as this charade suddenly felt like a crime against nature. She could feel the eyes of the assembled company, hard and curious, on them as well now. Those members of the *ton* tempted here by a delicious farce clearly hoped for some tasty gossip to take home with them at the end of this vulgar display, and what a delightful scandal they would have to chew on when they found out what Lady Fetherall had done to avoid marrying one of their favourite proud aristocrats.

'It will be my pleasure, Lady Fetherall,' he lied with such a blankly frozen look she almost wanted to laugh at the spectacle they must make—him so starkly elegant and her so tawdry and flirtatious in her sister's deepest scarlet gown.

The urge died as she felt something unwanted stir again deep down at the touch of his gloved hand on hers. He raised a haughty eyebrow at Tolbourne to say, *What are you waiting for? It's time to signal the orchestra to begin.* Then the viscount could get one more act of this tedious farce over and done with. Maybe he would drink himself into oblivion to blot out the distasteful prospect of marrying her at the end of it. She hoped so; he probably deserved to have the devil of a head for most of the next week for daring to think Caro actually wanted to marry him.

'Celine says I cannot wear white for a second marriage, my lord, but I don't see why not,' she made herself prattle as Lord Elderwood held her hand with only the very tips of his fingers; she longed to shout at him that poor taste and low breeding were not commonly thought to be catching. Instead, she forced herself to dance so jauntily that he would be too distracted by the view to wonder at any change he perceived in his bride-to-be.

Don't expect too much. Don't argue or disagree. And whatever you do, don't let anyone know you have a mind of your own and might consider doing something of which the males in control of your life would not approve.

Remembering this advice made Martha furious all over again, but it also helped her to fight her shivers of awareness when Lord Elderwood's hard body pressed too close as they moved through the figures of the dance.

Even in the melee that formed as other couples joined them on the floor, Lord Elderwood would know he had caused those shivers since it certainly wasn't cold in here. For once she was almost glad she wasn't wearing enough silk to keep a gnat warm as the heat of the room hit her full on the moment the dance was over.

All eyes seemed to be fixed on them again as he held on to her hand with a look of haughty disbelief. Martha saw the stubborn set of his chin and tight control of his nearly sensual mouth and knew in that moment that he must indeed be desperate for whatever Tolbourne had used to blackmail him into marrying Caro. What could he want so badly that he was willing to ignore his pride and logic and marry a woman he despised? It seemed to her that it was taking all his self-control not to call for his horse and gallop off into pounding rain and absolute darkness rather than endure another moment of this wretched farce.

Perhaps she could join him.

They could confess their real reasons for agreeing to the match as they made their way back to their everyday lives.

What a stupid idea, Martha. He would shun Caro's slandered and rejected half-sister even more than he does Caro herself.

She set her thoughts to imagining dark family secrets and Gothic horrors that might explain why Lord Elderwood had walked willingly into Tolbourne's web with his eyes wide open.

'I have won myself a great prize, Lady Fetherall,' he lied as he bowed slightly in her direction once again.

'You are too kind, my lord,' she lied back with a breathy titter.

'And your modiste is quite right, by the way. White would be completely out of the question for *your* second wedding,' he answered her earlier remark about a bridal gown with such a silky sneer it escaped their eager listeners. She thought to herself that she should thank him for the timely reminder to hate him.

'The pale rose satin she picked out suits me much better than the cold white of such a *virginal* gown anyway,' she said with a smile so sweet she hoped it would choke him.

'Yes, that hint of red will show you off so much better,' he said and she amused herself by picturing an even more outrageous gown than this one to wear at a wedding that was never going to happen.

He held her hand as if he had forgotten it was in his, though she couldn't quite bring herself to tug it free so publicly. She tried to stop herself trembling with nerves, but he gave her an examining look, as if he thought she was going to do something hysterical. He tucked her hand into the crook of his arm and that only made things worse. She was a widow, for goodness' sake—she knew what desire felt like and she didn't want to feel it for the likes of him. It was inexcusable for her inner wanton to imagine this man naked and rampantly aroused in her sister's bed for her very personal delight. Now she didn't even dare look at him in case he saw that wild fantasy in her eyes; obviously she had been widowed too long.

At least the thought of her beloved late husband reminded her that she was a woman who expected a lot more than a fine masculine face and form from her lover. She expected to be his everything, just as she and Tom had been to one another. She would never even be a *something* to Lord Elderwood.

'Shall I send for your maid?' he asked her as if he was surprised a human being lived inside Lady Fetherall's scandalous skin.

Martha wanted to slap him now, so that was better, wasn't it? 'I was merely a little overcome by the heat in here, but this is far too important a night for me to want to miss any of it, my lord,' she replied breathily and made herself cling to his arm as she wriggled as much bare skin against his powerful body as she could. She hoped the wanton display would disgust him.

'Then of course you must not do so, my lady,' Lord Elderwood said flatly.

Martha could not let herself regret meeting him like this, when they were bringing out the worst in one another. Lords did not hobnob with the grand-daughters of impoverished squires who had been bastardised by their own kin, and Mrs Lington, as she was now, only had time to play charades between harvest and the worst of a harsh northern winter that was due to blast its way in any day now. The hardships and rewards, the shared purpose of landowner, farmer and shepherd were her real life. Soon she would have to return to it and she would be much too busy to think of a haughty stranger with ice blue eyes and the face and form of an ancient Norse god.

Zach felt thoroughly confused yet oddly protective of this contrary woman at his side. He had spent so little time with her until now that he had no real idea who she really was under the paint and outrageous gowns. An unmarried viscount with any sense steered clear of women like her. He had long ago noted that she was beautiful, but that was only a lucky harmony of face and form bestowed by Mother Nature. A lesser woman would look ridiculous in such a gown but she didn't. How he wished she would stand further away! His determination to make sure Tolbourne never got his noble great-grandson via him felt shakier than it had before she had sauntered downstairs and watched him with such wariness that even he began to wonder if she was quite safe in his company. Her hand on his arm felt stronger than he had expected it to as she nestled it into the crook of his arm. He frowned at the mismatch between her fragile appearance, which spoke of idleness, and the slender strength of the limb now resting against his.

He reminded himself that she was a social climber, a predator in petticoats—and Fetherall's widow into the bargain. That seemed a long enough list of reasons why he should stick to his plan and walk away from her the moment their wedding was over and the documents were signed. Yet when he felt her tense at the approach of one of Tolbourne's cronies come to solicit her hand for the next dance, that list slipped clean out of his head. The fat old lecher let his lusty gaze fix on her richly curved breasts as if he had a right to leer at her and maybe more. Zach could see the man's stubby fingers flexing as if he had already got his hands on her body; she flinched and shifted even closer to Zach as if he was the lesser of two evils.

'Lady Fetherall has promised all her dances to me until we are wed,' he told the old lecher coldly.

'Thank you,' she murmured when the man muttered something that could be an apology for intruding on an engaged couple and went away again.

Zach wondered why she made herself so vulnerable to men like that by dressing the way she did. What purpose could she have now that they were engaged and she had her fish on the line? He didn't have time to ask her before Tolbourne appeared and said, 'I want his goodwill to sign a contract,' as if Zach weren't even present.

'Then you will have to get it by other means, won't you,' he said stiffly and felt Lady Fetherall flinch even closer to him at Tolbourne's silent threat of retribution if she didn't dance with a randy old man for the sake of his business.

'A nice little squeeze of warm, young flesh is all

the old fool wants,' Tolbourne said, as if her feelings about that repellent notion were irrelevant.

'The lady is *my* warm, young, affianced bride and I don't share,' Zach said with all the menace he could inject into his murmured words.

'You'll do as you're bid, my lad.'

'No, old man, I will not,' Zach told him blandly.

'I've got your trump card.'

'No, I've got yours,' Zach argued. 'And what I have I hold,' he added, holding up their joined hands so the man could see the most ostentatious Chilton family jewel flashing on Lady Fetherall's ring finger like the evil eye.

'You can't fight me! I can give you forty years,' the man blustered.

Of course he couldn't, but Zach wanted Tolbourne to think he might, if he were to be pushed too far. 'And several stone in weight, but that would only hasten my victory.'

'I can forbid the marriage,' Tolbourne blustered.

'And lose the title you have chased so hard and for so long? Sir Ambrose never did fulfil your dream of a noble great-grandson to boast about, did he?'

'And you will?'

'Do you doubt me?' Zach said haughtily.

'Make sure you get on with it post-haste, then,' Tolbourne demanded even as he backed away.

Zach felt an unpleasant squirm of guilt because he had no intention of doing anything of the sort. Tolbourne must not be able to use his granddaughter so cynically when she was married to him. At least now the old man seemed to believe Zach could really be dangerous if he was pushed too far and that would have to do, for now.

Chapter Three

Martha was so shocked by her latest insight into Caro's life here that she wanted to cling to Lord Elderwood's rock like a drowning man for the rest of the evening. Harmsley had to be offering Caro a better life and all his love and devotion, she thought, because her beautiful, gentle sister clearly deserved it. Martha hurt on her sister's behalf while she clung to the man their despicable grandfather had chosen for Caro.

'Remember why you're marrying her,' Tolbourne said.

Martha wondered—and not for the first time—precisely why that was as her grandfather eyed Lord Elderwood warily.

'A *gentleman's* word is his bond,' Lord Elderwood drawled.

'Make sure you keep it, then,' the old man snapped as he walked away. Of course he thought he must always have the final word.

'Thank you,' she murmured as they watched him walk away.

Martha thought Tolbourne would be more careful how he treated her—as long as he thought she was Caro—until the wedding that wasn't going to happen. The viscount had claimed those dances, for which she was grateful. She dared not consider what else he might claim before the wedding…perhaps a kiss? She could not allow it. That would be a deception too far and she refused to even think about how it might feel if the viscount wanted her in return.

'My pleasure,' Lord Elderwood replied with a real bow this time.

'He can be very dangerous,' she warned him.

'Only if he finds a weak spot to exploit,' Lord Elderwood said confidently, as if he were too well armoured to worry about Tolbourne's scheming. But he couldn't be, could he? If he was then he wouldn't have ended up engaged to Caro and gruff as a bear with a sore paw about it.

'He must have found yours, then,' she had to remind him, because neither of them could afford to forget how devious the old man was.

'Indeed,' he said stiffly, 'and having used it he has lost his advantage.'

'He will always try to control everyone connected to him by fair means or foul,' she said. But Elderwood wasn't going to marry Caro, so why was she bothering to issue that warning? Now he was watching her as if he had never truly seen her before— which of course he had not.

'Why *did* you return here when your husband died, my lady?' he said, as if he really was curious. Quite honestly, she wondered the same thing. 'You must have known he would take over your life as soon as you stepped over his threshold again.'

'Brose was very extravagant and left me very little to live on,' she improvised. The late Sir Ambrose was notorious for his loose lifestyle and excessive drinking so it seemed like a safe bet. 'And my grandfather has his own ways of getting people do what he wants,' she added cautiously. The viscount must know that himself by now since he was engaged to marry a woman he obviously didn't know from Adam, since he had not spotted that his bride had been swapped for her sister.

'That sounds to me like a very good reason *not* to put yourself back in his power, Lady Fetherall. Don't you think you would have been happier and safer with another family member—the supposed half-sister Tolbourne still refuses to acknowledge, for example—even if it meant a reduction in style and situation?'

'I could hardly ask her relations to take me in when we share no blood and they have no obligation towards me,' she said with a shrug, though of course that was a lie. 'And I thought that old scandal had been forgotten,' she added carelessly, hoping he couldn't feel the tension in her body as she said it since they were still too close for comfort.

'Of course I have made it my business to find out

everything I could about you as we are going to be married next week, Lady Fetherall.'

Not too much, I hope, she thought, but only said, 'What did you discover, my lord?' as if it was almost a joke that he had taken the trouble to find out more about Caro.

'Surprisingly little about your half-sister since Lakeland folk are so close-mouthed with nosy strangers and her family seem popular with their neighbours. Apparently nobody was keen to gossip about them.'

'I would not know since I am a stranger up there myself,' she made herself say with a shrug. 'I was only four when Grandfather sent her packing and he forbade all contact between us from that moment on for the sake of my reputation.'

'Really?' he said, looking startled that Caro thought she had a reputation left to protect. 'But you are a widow now, Lady Fetherall. Don't you want to know if the girl you once thought of as your sister is at least well and happy?'

'I dare not cross my grandfather in order to seek her out,' Martha murmured, as if she truly thought the old man had eyes and ears everywhere. Thank goodness that wasn't quite true, since Caro and Martha's plan had worked, so far. 'Since you have claimed my hand for the evening, shall we two sit down together and have a fine coze until supper is served, my lord?' she asked him with what she hoped was the same false brightness with which her sister usually deflected such uncomfortable questions.

'As you wish,' he said dully.

She should congratulate herself now that he was looking at her as if he would rather be outside in the rain than sitting out most of the dances with such a self-centred female. He thought his bride was a coward, which put her well and truly back on the other side of the chasm between her and the real man under his stiff facade. That should feel good. It was so much safer than wanting impossible things with such a powerful aristocrat. No good could come of that.

It *should* feel good, but somehow it didn't.

She felt stupidly touched that he had bothered to find out if the Tolbourne family skeleton was still alive. She ought to be in a panic because someone might have described her to his nosy stranger as closely resembling Caro. Her disguise had been good enough to fool everyone so far, and there was no point worrying when it seemed so unlikely he would give Mrs Martha Lington another thought.

The rest of the evening turned out to be a curious mixture of boredom, fear and the fine tension caused by her secret, guilty awareness of Lord Elderwood as a man. After a week of being drilled until she moved and spoke as languidly as a lady of fashion and after the tension of fearing someone would see through her disguise, she should have slept like a baby, but she didn't. The worry that she and Noakes had suffered during the journey to her grandfather's house from London today, as they constantly expected their carriage to be halted and both of them ordered to account for themselves since Caro had been caught trying to flee to Scotland with her lover, refused to relax its grip. If she had been able to forget that horror story, then Lord Elderwood's hint that he had had Caro investigated would have kept her tossing and turning until some ridiculous hour of the night.

When she did finally manage to fall asleep, an old nightmare pushed even thoughts of His Lordship out of her head. In the dream, she knew her screams and frantic pleas not to be parted from her little sister would be ignored but she couldn't help making them. Little Caro would be lost and so alone without her big sister to help her understand what was happening, but Tolbourne wrenched them apart and Martha was thrown into the already moving carriage like a piece of baggage. Caro's screams and wild weeping as she was parted from the last safe piece of her shattered world had haunted Martha ever since.

The horrid memories of that day when both of them had been too small to argue with the man she refused to call *Grandfather* were still with her when she woke to a reluctant January dawn. She felt even more determined to make this masquerade work as she imagined how poor Caro must have felt when Martha was bundled out of the house and she was left here alone with the wicked old man who was intent on making her obey his every order without question.

Maybe she had needed a terrifying reminder of why this charade was so important. Never mind Lord Elderwood's pride and the crushing blow to his self-respect when he found out he had been royally duped at the end of the week. Her sister had to have her chance to build a family of her own with the man of her choice. So Martha would keep pretending she was Caro, and Lord Elderwood would have to look after himself. Caro needed to marry her Mr Harmsley.

Martha was surprised how much she had liked the man when he evaded Tolbourne's watchers by dressing as a footman who had been sent to pick up some stylish piece of finery from Celine's exclusive establishment one day while Martha and Caro were busy rehearsing her part. She only had to see her sister's eyes go dreamy the moment she realised who the intruder really was to know he was the right man for her sister. Mr Harmsley might have been careless enough to get her sister with child well before their furtive elopement, but he had clearly fallen as hard for Caro as she had for him.

Feeling a little better about waking up in Caro's bed in this gaudy house, she reminded herself why she was here and then rang the bell for Noakes. Caro's maid took one look at the dark shadows under Martha's eyes and tutted her disapproval then told her to go back to bed. Martha knew she wouldn't sleep even if she did as she was told but agreed with Noakes's suggestion that an early-morning ride might put the roses back in her cheeks. She donned Caro's beautifully cut riding habit, thankful that even Tolbourne couldn't order one made by anyone except a London tailor if he wanted Caro to be considered fashionable. It was the only garment of her sister's she would have gladly taken back to Greygil with her at the end of this fiasco if she could. She refused to take anything from the man who had caused so much misery to so many, even if she had had any use for such a fine garment in her busy life.

When she got to the stable yard, Martha was shocked to see the very man who had tossed her into that moving carriage nearly twenty years ago come towards her as if he thought Caro would be pleased to see him. He certainly greeted her like an old friend; she must have said something right since he went off to fetch her mare with a cheerful promise not to be long.

So Martha sat and brooded about that awful day in this very stable yard all those years ago and shuddered at the memory of the world gone mad around her. Grown-up Martha tried to reason with herself. The under groom, as he must have been back then, would have lost his job if he had refused to toss the struggling, kicking little Martha into the carriage to begin the long journey north without her sister. It was still hard for grown-up Martha to be fair to the man who had done that despite the agonised screams of both her and Caro. She had tried to live down the shame and slander of being branded a bastard behind her grandparents', and protective Tom Lington's, backs but the truth was it haunted her to this day, especially at odd, painful moments like this one when she was reminded of that awful day when her and her sister's lives were changed forever.

That was why she was sitting on the mounting

block in Caro's stylish riding habit while she waited for Caro's horse to be brought out after refusing a dry seat in the tack room instead. She frowned at her own folly now that last night's rain threatened to seep through the cushion the man had insisted on fetching for her to sit on out here. It still felt impossible for her to be sensible after her nightmare had replayed the pain of the past so vividly. Though maybe the blame for her largely sleepless and dream-haunted night wasn't entirely due to her lingering memories of Tolbourne parting her from Caro and sending her away with his horrible accusations about her mother ringing in her ears. She had used it to block out the new nightmare that had come after it. Now a fresh horror was haunting her and she dearly wished it would vanish into the ether and stop there.

The terrible truth was that Lord Elderwood had taken Tom's place in her dearest but most hopeless fantasy and she was still horrified by it. She hated her unconscious mind for betraying her and her beloved late husband like that. It was true that the real Lord Elderwood had been a shock to her. He was so unexpected, so close to a more naive woman's version of manly perfection that she supposed many women had entertained such dreams of him; some would even have achieved their dearest fantasy of having him as their lover. He was obviously deeply offended by being forced to marry Caro, thanks to some cunning threat known only to him and Tolbourne, and it made him Martha's worst nightmare.

Yet his spectre had satisfied her deepest, darkest

fantasies of a lover last night, and she could not rec-
oncile the fact that he had taken Tom's place in her
dreams. It must be a symptom of having pretended
to be Caro, she tried to convince herself. Last night
she had been so tense with nerves it was little wonder Lord Elderwood had intruded on her favourite
dream of Tom, warm and sensual and real in their big
bed at Greygil as he would never be again in real life.

She had got used to missing Tom when he was at
sea, but this was complete loss for he would never
return. After loving Tom, she knew how driven and
glorious mutual desire could be, but she would never
have it again, for Tom Lington had been the love of
her life. The Viscount Elderwood who had been passionate, urgent and ardent last night in her dreams
was a lie. He didn't even like Caro very much and
would certainly not want Martha if he knew it was
her standing in Caro's shoes, deceiving and humiliating him as thoroughly as she could for as long as
she could while her sister got away.

She eyed the stable doors sourly and wondered
why it was taking so long for the grooms to saddle
one single mare. She expected more haste in a house
where servants went about on tiptoe for fear of their
master's wrath. She wondered what those servants
said about Tolbourne behind his back. Did they mut-
ter complaints about his cold brusqueness and whisper that he had been born a pauper so what right did
he have to order them about like cattle? *The right of
money*, Martha thought cynically, but she couldn't
help hoping some of them quietly despised the hard

man they were paid to serve. Yet the groom was still here after all these years so perhaps they simply took Tolbourne's money and did as they were bid. Right now she wished they were in awe of Caro as well because she needed a vigorous ride on a willing horse to get these stupid images of Lord Elderwood as the impassioned lover out of her head before she had to act as his unwanted fiancée again to his face.

'Good morning, Lady Fetherall,' the deep voice she least wanted to hear greeted her from too nearby and almost made her jump out of her skin.

'Oh! Good morning, Lord Elderwood,' she managed to reply as her heart raced with panic and shock at the contrast between the lover in her dreams and the uncomfortable reality in front of her.

His icy blue eyes focused sharply on her as if he were trying to get the true measure of his bride-to-be. She fervently hoped that he never would. Goodness knows what he saw because he nodded his head a greeting and gave her a guarded look.

'You were so lost in thought I began to wonder if I might have to bellow before you took any notice,' he said. 'Maybe I should have worn hobnailed boots to warn you I was on my way,' he said with a faint twist of humour she wished he'd kept to himself.

'I don't think they would match your elegant riding attire, my lord. And do you actually possess such a thing as hobnail boots?'

'Will you jilt me if I lay claim to a pair, my lady?'

'Probably not,' she replied with a sigh, because

Caro would not dare and Martha couldn't step outside this stupid masquerade and do it for her.

There was a moment of awkward silence while they both rubbed against the thorny facts of this marriage promise between them. If he but knew that neither she—nor Caro—wanted the match any more than he did, what would he think?

'Was you meaning to ride as well, Your Lordship?' the flustered-looking head groom questioned from the door to the stables. 'Only, Her Ladyship's mare's gone lame. I'm that sorry I hadn't noticed before we went to put your saddle on her, my lady.' The man actually sounded genuinely sorry and Martha warmed towards him despite their uncomfortable past history.

'Is there anything else already brought in that you think would suit for me?' she asked him, because he knew Caro's capabilities better than she did.

'The roan gelding's a sweet goer so you could try him, Your Ladyship, and I'll get the mare to the farrier double quick so she's ready for you to ride tomorrow.'

'No, don't do that. It would fluster her and I don't want her to be any more upset than she must be already. If you will just have my saddle put on the gelding, we will see how we two get along for the next couple of days.'

Martha could not recall the man's name, but she was sure Noakes or Caro must have told her, along with all the other names she was supposed to memorise so nobody would suspect she wasn't Caro. If

Lord Elderwood would just go away so she could recall her lessons without him here to distract her from them, she was sure it would come to her soon.

'My horse needs a good rest after his journey here so if you have something up to my weight I will accompany Lady Fetherall on her ride and make sure she is safe on a strange mount.'

'Safe on anything in our stables except the devil you rode in on, Her Ladyship is, my lord,' the head groom argued as if he was none too sure even a viscount deserved Caro's hand in marriage.

Martha had to stare down at her riding boots to hide her surprise that this particular man seemed devoted to her half-sister. She only recalled his hard hands lifting her up as she fought and screamed and his harsh voice ordering her to stop frightening the horses. Perhaps he had been harsh to hide his real feelings about having to do such a terrible thing, or perhaps Caro had charmed him afterwards. Her sweet-tempered but painfully shy little sister was still there behind Lady Fetherall's blank social smile and wary eyes.

Martha liked to think that Graves's—for that was his name, she now recalled—hard heart was softened by pity for the lonely little girl Caro must have been when she was growing up here. Maybe he was the one who had taught her to ride so well. Yes, now she remembered it, his name was Graves, and as he seemed to be Caro's friend she would remember it from now on.

'I taught Her Ladyship to ride so I should know,'

Graves said, confirming her suspicions with a slightly puzzled look at Martha. She must remember to play her part with him a lot better than she had done so far.

'And taught me so well I can outride most folk, can't I, Graves?'

'I did my best but you was always a natural, Miss Caro. Game as they come, Her Ladyship is in the saddle, m'lord,' Graves said with an assessing, almost warning glance at Lord Elderwood before he went off to order the gelding saddled and something suitable for a gentleman to ride.

'Does your grandfather ride, Lady Fetherall?' Elderwood asked as they waited.

'Hardly at all,' she replied with a slight smile to say maybe that was why Graves had been so keen to make sure Caro did it so well.

'Your groom makes me feel as if I am only here on approval,' Elderwood observed wryly.

'Never mind. I doubt he has the power to get you sent back to the House of Lords if you prove unsatisfactory, my lord.'

'I dare say not; I'm not sure they would want me,' he replied coolly, as if she had reminded him he was being bought like a commodity.

'Why not?'

'I have spoken about subjects they would prefer me to be silent about,' he said tersely. She would have loved to ask more, but his closed expression said he didn't want to talk about his causes, whatever they were, and maybe Caro ought to know about them already.

'So what were you really thinking about just now?' he asked as if he was determined to change the subject.

'Oh, nothing much. Just brooding on the past, I suppose,' she said truthfully.

'Only the sad parts of it, from your wistful expression.'

Chapter Four

How careless of her to forget who she was here even for a few moments when so much depended on her being Caro in everything but fact for six more days. For some odd reason she longed to confide in this strong man, to tell him the truth about Martha Lington and her life from the inside out, and Caro's as well. She wanted him to know the truth about her parents' marriage and Tolbourne's foul slander of her mother. She wanted him to know that Caro was a good woman whose life had been bent out of shape by her own grandfather and her late husband.

Before she left this place and all this pretence behind her, she wanted Lord Elderwood to know the truth about the Tolbourne sisters instead of Squire Tolbourne's lies. But for now, she could not put Caro's escape in jeopardy even if it seemed as if he genuinely wanted to hear the truth about the woman he had promised to marry—and she was quite sure that it was the last thing he was going to want when he found out about the deception.

'All of us have a few unhappy memories, don't we, my lord?' she said carefully.

'Aye,' he said thoughtfully, and Martha made herself look away because she had no right to ask about any of his.

She gazed at the rich countryside around them instead, and made herself think about the differences between this place and the land she knew so well in the Lakes. It stopped her wondering what Lord Elderwood's homeland was like and what sort of life he lived there. She tried to picture the orchards in full bloom and lush grass growing in the meadows, which it would do here, a mere half a day from sooty old London, weeks before spring would arrive at Greygil.

She told herself she didn't want to know what the viscount made of this house and the land around it that he could expect to inherit one day through this hateful marriage to Tolbourne's heiress. She could not picture him living a soft life here. He seemed to belong to higher, harder places somehow—moors and dales perhaps. She could see him riding across those moors or striding rough hill country for hours on end, narrowing his steely blue eyes to assess what should change and what could remain wild and barely touched by the hand of man.

His gaze felt uncomfortably perceptive as he shook off whatever sad memories were haunting him and narrowed his eyes on her again. That would teach her to think too hard about what kind of man he was and what kind of husband he would be when he was here to catch her doing it.

'You must be cold after sitting up there for so long at this time of year,' he said.

'Maybe I am a little, but here come Graves and the stable lads with the horses so I shall soon warm up when I'm in the saddle,' she said with a sigh of relief she hoped he would not hear above the noise of iron-shod hooves on the cobbles.

She realised Graves was not exaggerating when he claimed Caro was a fine horsewoman as soon as she saw the fine animal he was leading. The roan was carrying a lady's saddle and dancing about as if he was very full of oats and raring to be off. Graves must think Caro could handle him but Martha wasn't so sure *she* could. She was used to hill ponies and Grandfather Winton's stubborn old cob. She was just glad the gelding wasn't Caro's usual mount so he was less likely to sense the difference between them and play up. Martha had quite enough to worry about without coping with a nervous and restless horse that sensed things humans couldn't. Her main priority was not to fall off or let the horse or Lord Elderwood know she was nowhere near as confident in the saddle as Caro would be.

'Are you feeling any warmer yet?' Lord Elderwood asked as they trotted up the bridleway. It was an effort to hold her eager mount back but she was beginning to relax in her sister's saddle and believe she could do this.

'Much more so, I thank you,' she said politely. It wasn't his fault she had longed to escape from all the lying for an hour or so and ride out on her own.

It felt odd to be fussed over again when nobody ever thought to ask Mrs Lington if she was warm enough in layers of serge and flannel and the sturdy boots that were never quite waterproof enough on the fells. Everyone took it for granted that she knew what she was doing and would be as well protected from a Cumberland winter as a person could be. What would this fastidious nobleman make of her true self, bundled in as many layers as she could wear without them weighing her down? No doubt he would be shocked at her willingness to stride the hills to make sure the sheep were safe and that the shepherds had whatever fuel and help they needed to tend them.

Grandfather still insisted on farming the Home Farm himself, despite Grandmama's pleas to let it out and take the rent. Martha knew he wanted to make her own life more secure because she said she would not remarry. The profits were being added to the small fortune Grandfather meant to leave her one day, but she said she would far rather he was comfortable and stopped worrying about her future.

'Your horse looks as if he's eager for a race,' Elderwood said, as if he wanted to pit her lively mount against his.

All of a sudden she longed to know what his real name was. It felt odd to even think about him as Lord Elderwood when there seemed to be a man of character under the stiff pride after all. She could hardly refuse his half-offered invitation for a good gallop when Caro's abilities in the saddle were apparently common knowledge. When they were children, Martha would ride races against Tom on the flatter parts of the fells as they pretended to be on high-bred racehorses instead of tough fell ponies. Maybe she hadn't quite forgotten how to do it after all this time, although she was on a ladylike side-saddle instead of astride and her horse was probably twice the size of her adored childhood pony.

'Your grey is bigger but I am lighter so I suppose we could test their paces and not send them back to their stables nearly as full of oats as they were when we set out,' she agreed recklessly.

She would soon find out if she remembered how it felt to race as fast as her horse could go to beat her best friend. But this man wasn't her friend, was he? There would be no urchin grin and teasing at the end of it, or the glint of more-complicated feelings in Tom's still boyish face when they got older and began to notice the changes maturity was bringing to their friendship. She blinked back a tear for those lost and carefree days and shook her head to pull herself out of the past. It was time she put them further behind her; maybe she could even forget she was a grieving widow for the next few days, until Caro was safe.

'True,' Lord Elderwood said and raised an eyebrow as if he was waiting for her signal to be off. 'I will give you a head start,' he offered and she glared at him before she had even thought of what Caro might do. But her sister wasn't here and for once she was going to do what Martha wanted—and she wanted to gallop headlong and not be treated like a weakling.

'If you do I shall turn around and ride straight back to the stables,' she challenged him with a not very Caro frown to say *You dare*.

'Neck and neck it is, then,' he agreed with a cocky grin. Suddenly it felt like a real race and she was determined to win it.

'Let's get on with it, then,' she said as if he had been keeping her waiting, and waved her hand like the starter on a rac course.

Lady Fetherall was off before he hardly had time to urge his horse into the gallop he had been itching for since the grey emerged from his stable. Zach was tempted not to try very hard to win as the sight of Lady Fetherall swaying lithely to the movement of her horse tugged at something he didn't want to think about. There wasn't just the risk of a physical arousal he was mature enough to keep under control most of the time; it felt as if there was the threat of something deeper and a lot more dangerous in the sharp winter air this morning. It was because she looked freer than he had ever seen her look before, he decided—young and reckless and nothing like the predatory widow he had thought her when Tolbourne had made her sound as if she was willing to do anything to get a viscountess's coronet on her head.

He was beginning to doubt his first impression,

and realised his prejudice had made it easier to plan that unpleasant trick on her after the wedding. Part of him didn't want to let go of that prejudice, because it felt like a kind of protection and a comfort for being forced into the marriage in the first place.

'You're an idiot, Elderwood,' he murmured and the grey's ears flicked back to gauge his rider's mood. If Zach allowed a fleeting desire for this woman to overcome his common sense, he was going to lose a lot more than this race. He should take her superficial appearance as an indication of the empty ambition that lay beneath it and forget she might be anything more.

'Come on, then, bonny lad,' he urged the powerful animal and rose in his stirrups to crouch over the grey's neck and give them the best advantage as the gentle rise flattened out. Now there was space to truly race against a lighter horse and rider, and for a moment they were neck and neck. He had to fight an urge to simply watch her lithe figure and intent face as she rode at his side as if every cell in her body was intent on beating him. Somehow he resisted the urge to gaze at her rather than at where he was going, but he was struck by the thought that she was not unlike the languid everyday version of Lady Fetherall he had seen so far. He doubted whether most of her acquaintances would even recognise her as this Diana in modern dress, with her face splashed with mud and all the life and fire she usually kept hidden making her look as truly magnificent as nature had intended her to be.

It felt private and almost secretive for him to see the real woman under the wispy draperies and cynical dark eyes. He told himself he wasn't here to gauge her thoughts, or wonder what colour her eyes were in daylight again as the grey lengthened his stride and gradually pulled ahead. It didn't help that he had an image of her striving so hard to beat him in mind now and listened for the concession she would have to make if they weren't going to ride all the way to Canterbury to prove his horse could outrun and outstay hers.

'Pax!' he finally heard her shout. 'We concede,' she added.

He risked a backward glance to watch her slowing the roan and telling him what a clever and wonderful horse he was. Stupid of him to feel jealous of a horse and yet here he still was, doing just that. He watched her croon endearments in the finely bred animal's ears so that the proud roan looked like he *had* won the race rather than lost it because his rider was so pleased with him. It appeared she had a generous soul and a kind heart under the showy armour. That probably wasn't a good thing for him to know, given what lay ahead of them in their marriage.

'It was hardly a fair race,' he made himself tell her casually. 'This fine lad is bigger and far more of a bruiser than your finely built roan.'

The grey was being ridden by a bruiser as well, Zach added in his head.

He immediately wished this week over so he could find Lady Fetherall a house in town and leave her there to hasten the time when an enterprising lover would take her fancy, thus enabling him to set his bride aside and regain his freedom. He couldn't deny that, since he was beginning to know her better, the thought of what he intended to do felt like staking the scapegoat out in the desert so the beasts could devour his sins along with the wretched victim. He felt like a beast himself because he still meant to do it. A true marriage between them would be a disaster. He couldn't inflict another one of those on his family after the havoc his grandmother's marriage to his rogue of a grandfather had inflicted on her and on Zach's father as well.

Then Lady Fetherall smiled openly at him for the first time, as if she had enjoyed this taste of freedom so much she couldn't help herself. He forgot his devious plan for a shocked moment and stared back at her. He realised now it was more than simple lust, and that was very dangerous indeed.

He used his mount's sudden attack of bad manners as an excuse to ride in front of her so he didn't have to watch her sway to the movement of her horse all the way back to Tolbourne's ugly modern house. The sight of Lady Fetherall free of her grandfather's control for once sparked off all sorts of impossible ideas in his head and he could not, *would not*, do as her grandfather wanted and sire heirs on her, no matter how much he wanted to now. He refused to be owned or driven by Tolbourne as her first husband had been. Zach Chilton would not march to the same tune as Brose Fetherall had, and he wondered how Lady Fetherall had managed to stay true to herself after being married to that sot for so long. He dismissed it as simple curiosity, nothing significant. He had his duty to do, and finding out about the real Lady Fetherall under the showy, grasping exterior would only make it harder.

'Looks like you've managed him perfectly, Your Ladyship,' the head groom told her when they were back in the stable yard. However, his gaze was sharp on Zach, as if he really was still on approval and had better watch his step with her.

'He's a fine lad, right as ninepence,' she said and slid out of the saddle before Zach could dismount and lift her down. That was a good thing, wasn't it? Better not to find out if his hands could span her narrow waist or risk making a fool of himself in front of her loyal supporter.

'Aye, and mine was a fine ride too, but now I must go and see how my own holy terror does this morning, if you will excuse me, my lady?'

'Yes, of course. I must change before any of my grandfather's guests are up and about,' she said with a rueful look at the groom, which Zach told himself he didn't envy in the slightest. He stood and watched her go as if he was as fascinated by Her Ladyship as an eager bridegroom should be.

'We moved your stallion to the other stable block, my lord. He didn't like being near another male, not even one of the geldings. Wouldn't rest until they was out of his sight and scent,' the head groom told him dourly.

'Aye, he's a ruffian,' Zach admitted with a fond smile for his fiery favourite. 'I should have brought a quieter hack but he'll happily go all day and I was in a hurry.' *In a hurry not to be here, if the truth be known*, and he had left it too late to get here by any other means and not be insultingly late for his own betrothal ball.

'He's a devil but I never saw a finer bit of blood and bone, Your Lordship.'

'Aye, he'll do,' Zach said and asked for directions to Thor's new stable.

Martha managed to avoid meeting Lord Elderwood in private for the rest of the day and she escaped to her room with the excuse of a headache that evening. Noakes made her drink a posset as if she really had that headache so Martha slept well and woke early enough to ride out with only Graves for company next morning.

Taking care not to be alone with Elderwood again meant she had to spend more time with Tolbourne and his restless and demanding guests than she wanted to, but she sighed and decided she couldn't have everything she wanted while she was living Caro's life for a while. She wondered why the social season was thought to be such a wonderful treat when it must mean mixing with spoilt and aimless people like these for months on end. She decided that the best and brightest of polite society were hardly likely to let themselves be lured to a cit's country house, even by the prospect of delicious gossip and all the luxuries Tolbourne's wealth could offer them.

After spending most of the day with those who had only been tempted here by the promise of gossip, the headache she had pretended last night was all too real. Tolbourne would never let Caro absent herself from hostess duties for two nights running so she would just have to grit her teeth and endure it. Somehow she had to keep Caro's social smile in place no matter how much she wanted to scream at the chattering guests to be quiet for once and allow her to suffer in silence.

So, how long *did* it take to drive a hired chaise to Scotland? Perhaps three days might do it in midsummer, with several changes of good horses a day and coachmen willing to drive for every hour of daylight. If it were summer she could possibly have set out on her own long journey home as soon as the household was safely asleep tonight, but as it was January there weren't enough hours of daylight to rely on Caro and Harmsley getting far enough to make a pursuit impossible, and the roads would be in a terrible state. Harmsley would be too concerned for Caro and the baby's safety to risk travelling on in darkness and there was not enough moonlight anyway.

She considered all the other hazards that might maroon them in the middle of nowhere if they were rash enough to try it. Not three days then—more like six or seven, she accepted gloomily. Even that would depend on there being no thrown horseshoes, no broken axle, no snapped traces, no running into someone who knew them.

Rumours that Lady Fetherall had learned how to be in two places at the same time could start up all too soon if that happened, but even if none of those hazards got in the way it was clear to Martha that she would have to stay here for as long as she could get away with it before the wedding. She bit back a heavy sigh at the thought of how much deception still lay ahead of her while the ladies chattered like magpies over the teacups in the drawing room after dinner.

She handed out tea like the perfect hostess, pretending she was quite unaware that most of them despised her—despised *Caro*. One or two were jealous of the fine catch Tolbourne's money had netted her sister—as if Elderwood were a particularly fine hound or a sleek fish or a prime piece of bloodstock, Martha thought scornfully. She went on passing out cups and managed not to pour tea over their spiteful, avaricious heads for Caro's sake. Of course, that was why she hated them—not on Elderwood's behalf or her own. He was hardly undefended; he could crush anyone he chose to with a hard look and a few well-chosen words. But maybe he wouldn't choose to.

He was a free man for five more nights. She had now spent two evenings here, and a third was almost over. Would Elderwood read the sleepy invitation in one or two of these fine ladies' eyes and let them console him for his forthcoming marriage to a cit's granddaughter? For all she knew, when the guests were supposed to be in their own chaste beds, he was stealing about the house in the stilly watches of the night, enjoying his last few nights of unwedded bliss. Tolbourne wouldn't care as long as Lord Elderwood turned up to marry his granddaughter on the appointed day. He would probably think more of him for enjoying himself before he got down to the serious business of getting his new wife with child.

For some odd reason, Martha's headache suddenly felt so much worse. The din in the room seemed deafening. If she didn't escape for a few moments she might scream and give the game away, so she murmured an excuse with a shrug at the teapot to say *No wonder I need some privacy after pouring so much tea* and slipped away.

None of the ladies would miss her if she was away for a little longer than usual; they hadn't noticed that she had taken her sister's place because they were all so wrapped up in their own dramas and concerns. There was a conservatory at the end of one of the quieter corridors and she slipped in there with a sigh of relief, hoping the gentlemen were too busy with port and warm stories to find it. Inside its glass doors it was blissfully dark with just enough warmth to keep the exotic plants alive through the winter. She looked round for a bench to enjoy the earthy aroma for a few moments.

'Lady Fetherall,' the deep voice she had been trying so hard not to listen out for rumbled from the darkest shadows, and she almost jumped out of her skin.

Drat the man but this was becoming a habit of his.

She should have felt his presence when she stole in here, although she supposed that explained why the fine hairs on the back of her neck had been prickling even as the headache began to release its iron grip.

'Lord Elderwood,' she said, surprised she didn't sound as close to the end of her tether as she felt.

'Meeting someone?' he asked cynically.

'No, are you?'

'No.' He sounded revolted by the very idea that he would meet a lover under Caro's nose.

'Were you blowing a cloud, then? I believe that's what you gentlemen call it.'

'No, filthy habit,' he said as if she were accusing him of something far worse than smoking a furtive cigarillo. 'I can't stand the taste.'

'Neither can I,' she replied, smiling in the darkness at the sharp memory of Tom smoking one during his last leave before Trafalgar, when she had told him it had better not become a habit. But he had had no time to develop one before he was felled during the battle, and she let herself be Tom Lington's widow again for a tender, aching moment of missing him in this steamy darkness. Grief flattened her smile at the memory of him being so sheepish about his new vice.

But she must turn her back on her real life or risk giving herself away. Acting a part was nine-tenths believing it, according to Caro, and she ought to know since she had been playing one for all her adult life.

'Ladies should not even try it,' Lord Elderwood told her disapprovingly.

'Ah, but I'm not one of those, am I?' she replied bitterly, thinking of the things so-called ladies whispered about Caro behind her back, things that made her glad to be unladylike Mrs Lington under the silk and paint and hair dye.

'What are you, then, my lady?'

'An ordinary being, striving to live a good enough life.'

'Really?' he drawled. 'I don't see many signs of hard work.'

He sounded more cynical than he had during the morning ride and she wondered whether she had offended him by avoiding him ever since? But surely he was happy to be kept at arm's length by his unwanted bride? Without being able to see more than his shadowy outline in the dark, there was no clue to how he was feeling except in his deep voice and this odd tension that seemed to tighten her nerves and tug at her senses whenever he was anywhere near her.

'That's the secret of it, you see, my lord,' she countered lightly as if she hadn't noticed the insult in his words. 'It takes work to hide what it costs me to be notorious and yet to seem not to care.'

'Yet you do it with such ease.'

'You don't know how much work it takes, though, do you, my lord? Since I'm so good at it,' she said, because she didn't think he had any right to cast stones at her little sister. 'You hear the gossip, despite pretending not to, and you sit in your ivory tower and judge what we lesser mortals do and say from afar. You have no idea what we truly hope and feel and strive for.'

'I'm not there now, though, am I?' he said gruffly and almost angrily.

'Where?'

'In my ivory tower,' he replied. Now he was so close, even in this fuggy darkness, that she knew he was looming over her and it felt deliciously dangerous to stay still and wait for whatever he said next.

'You have only come down from it temporarily to study my shortcomings at closer quarters, I dare say,' she said lightly, teasingly.

She was guiltily aware of the man beneath his lordly disguise tonight, and because she had to use her other senses he seemed more intriguing than ever in the gloom. She caught a trace of good soap and lemon water—of course he would have bathed and shaved before dinner, being such a gentleman, and that was a luxury of which she thoroughly approved. His breathing was slow and steady in the quiet and they seemed miles away from the chattering guests. She could walk away—he wasn't trapping her and the door was just behind her—yet she stood as if she had forgotten how to move and waited to see what he would do next with her heartbeat thundering in her ears and her breath coming so much shorter and shallower than his.

'Very much closer,' he said huskily and he was right, he was.

Chapter Five

Her shortcomings—that was what she had been talking about—but somehow his seemed more interesting. 'I don't care a snap of my fingers what you think of me, Lord Elderwood,' she lied nervously.

'Excellent. Then you won't mind if I do this,' he replied. He was so close now that she could feel his warmth, and she ignored the last bit of sanity screaming *Run!*

She licked her lips nervously. 'Don't you dare…' she began huskily but his mouth stopped her faint-hearted protest and he did dare.

Oh, yes, he definitely dared. Lord Elderwood's kiss was just as she had dreamed it would be. Exciting and befuddling, just like she thought it would be when she wondered about his inner poet and his not quite sensual mouth the first time she saw him. Her mouth softened under his without permission from the rest of her. She sighed into his questing mouth and knew she had been lonely for too long. It felt glo-

rious to be kissed with such sensual pleasure again
but with even more fire and intensity than she ever
had been before. Lord Elderwood was a mature man,
sure of himself and even a little bit arrogant, while
Tom had barely been twenty when he was killed. He
had been Martha's best friend as well as her lover
and she felt guilty now because she had never been
kissed quite like this before and she was enjoying
it too much.

Her knees had gone weak and her limbs heavy
with longing so she couldn't run away even if she
wanted to. Instead, she closed her eyes and was un-
faithful to her late husband's memory with a Viking
lover. Elderwood's strong and shapely hands were
the ones exploring her supple back with a lover's caress this time. She wriggled with delight at the feel of
his touch, so firm yet gentle and mesmerising. Tom's
wife should have reeled back in shock and pushed
him away by now, but instead, Martha keened softly
and opened her mouth to invite the invader in.

She opened her eyes, but even that didn't break
the spell as the shine of his hot, needy gaze looking back at her only fascinated her even more as he
plunged his tongue into her mouth. She tangled hers
with his and they watched each other as her insides
threatened to melt and she had to lean against his en-
circling arms for support. Mrs Lington didn't even
want to push wanton Martha aside and demand this
stop right now, not with the viscount's mouth on hers
and his eyes watching her as he kissed her as though
he would only ever want her. They were sharing such

hungry intimacy in the quiet darkness, but he didn't know who he was really kissing.

He thought she was Caro; he thought she was his future wife. Confusion ran into need and said she had to be glad when he drew back from their sense-stealing kiss as if he had heard the confusion of her mind. There was just enough light to see him stare down at her as if he wanted to read every thought in her head. Heaven forbid, because there was no excuse for what she had done but it still felt exciting and dangerous here, with him. He didn't seem to want to let her go and she didn't pull further away. She tried to picture all the lovers he must have already known and walked away from, but even that didn't work because right now he wanted *her* and she definitely wanted him.

She wanted to be seduced and pleasured until she forgot why it was so wrong and in so many ways. She longed for Elderwood to trail slow kisses down her very bare neck and whisper a deliciously admiring touch over her aching breasts. She went hot and shivery with need at the very thought of his strong but elegant long fingers on her bare skin. Now she longed to push herself even closer to his gently demanding touch and silently beg him to tease and caress her starkly aroused nipples to even more desperation. Wouldn't it feel wonderful to murmur soft encouragement for him to do even more wondrous things to her while she went wild in his arms? Yes, it would feel wonderful, but the idea of being caught wanton and exposed with a man she met two days ago shocked her into taking that step back from him at long last.

She wasn't really this haughty nobleman's eager betrothed; she was Tom Lington's widow. Tom would be so disappointed if she became intimate with a man who didn't love her as fervently and completely as he always had.

Maybe wanton Martha did still want to seize the ultimate in pleasure with such a powerful lover for as many nights as they had left here, but wanton Martha would have to want in vain. Need and loneliness still clamoured inside her and she had to turn away from Lord Elderwood's intent gaze as she fought this outrageous need for more. She gasped in a long, unsteady breath and waited for him to call her a tease—or worse. She hated being so fickle. Maybe she had clung too hard to her grief and the memory of her lost love, but she couldn't use Elderwood to ward off bitter loneliness and an empty bed. It wouldn't be fair, to either of them. His breathing sounded ragged as well and it must be costing him a mighty effort to force his protesting body back under stern control again, but he did it anyway. She had to admire him for doing it in tense silence rather than cursing and swearing and stamping about, but maybe she would feel less tense if he hadn't gone quite so still while he fought a private battle.

'I'm sorry,' she said, 'I had the headache,' she added ineptly.

'Again?'

'Last night I was lying; tonight it's the truth,' she

said with as much dignity as she could, under the circumstances.

'Even more so now, I suspect. I'm sorry too,' he said with a heavy sigh.

'If I hadn't lied last night I could have gone to bed early and nobody would have thought anything of it, but I did, so I came in here for some peace and quiet instead. I should never have lied.'

'No wonder you did, if that's the sort of thing I do to you when you risk being alone with me.'

'Would *anyone* have done? Would you have kissed any woman who came in here alone?' she was horrified to hear herself ask him.

'Unfortunately not,' she thought she heard him say but she must have been wrong.

'Unfortunately?' she echoed with a bewildered shake of her head.

'Did I say that? I meant *fortunately*, of course,' he corrected hastily.

What a pair of liars they were—him pretending he was glad he wanted her and her pretending to be her half-sister. 'We both know you don't want to marry me, Lord Elderwood,' she said cooly.

'What if we don't?'

'Don't what?'

'Don't marry one another.'

'My grandfather would be furious, although I doubt that would worry you much,' she said carefully. If they didn't play out this farce at least until their supposed wedding day, this whole sorry business would unravel and Caro could still be caught.

Yet there was a part of her that was hurt he had followed up that kiss with a suggestion that they decide not to marry. He wouldn't be marrying her in any case, but he didn't know it.

'He would take it out on you, wouldn't he?' he said.

This was deep water indeed and he sounded as if he cared that Tolbourne very likely would lash out at her if he were thwarted. She didn't want to know about Viscount Elderwood's gentler side; she didn't need more excuses to find him ridiculously attractive. She wasn't Lady Fetherall and he wasn't going to marry her.

'As you pointed out only the other day, I am of age and a widow,' she told him as expressionlessly as she could manage. 'I could walk away from Tolbourne House any time I choose to.'

'Then why don't you?'

Yes, why not, Caro? Martha silently asked her absent sister but she knew the answer. Until she had met Harmsley, Caro had simply done whatever Tolbourne told her to; that was how she had been raised. Well, it wouldn't be Caro's future; a better future for her sister was the truth behind Martha's lies, so she would just have to learn to lie better.

'This place is my home,' she told him.

'Not for much longer,' he said but she had already smoothed down her skirts and turned back in the direction of Caro's guests and a more everyday kind of lying.

'I bid you goodnight, my lord. Maybe you could

take your turn at having the headache tonight and spare us an awkward encounter in the drawing room,' she said distantly and didn't wait for a reply.

His absence and a terse message via the butler to say His Lordship had urgent estate matters to deal with told her he had found a better way to avoid her. The rest of the evening dragged because he wasn't there and her headache felt miserable. She was so relieved when she could finally bid the guests goodnight and sit still while Noakes took out all the hairpins that were sticking into her scalp and gently brushed out her curls.

'You're a good girl, Miss Martha,' Noakes told her unexpectedly.

'You never said so when Caro and I were little.'

'You were a little scallywag, always getting Miss Caro into trouble.'

'Is that why you stayed with her?'

'Your nanny couldn't stay after ripping up at the old devil for calling you a bastard. Miss Caro needed somebody to love her and he was never going to.'

'True.'

'Only loves himself, that one,' Noakes said with her most fearsome frown.

'True again.'

'It'll be a glad day for us all when Her Ladyship marries her true love and it will be thanks to you, Miss Martha.'

'At least I will have done something to atone for causing so much trouble for you all when we were little, then,' Martha said lightly, but she was glad when Noakes finished plaiting her hair for the night and left her to try to sleep with all that was racing around in her head with a much gentler goodnight than usual.

Martha felt confused and deeply troubled as she got into Caro's showy feather bed and hoped she would not dream of a lordly lover again tonight. Lord Elderwood could still catch Caro and her lover on that great stallion Graves had told her about this morning. Mental pictures of the viscount riding like the devil to drag poor Caro back, after flinging all sorts of bitter allegations at Martha, span around in her head as she finally drifted into an exhausted sleep. She awoke determined to do everything she possibly could to keep this deception going and try her hardest to make sure she was never alone with Lord Elderwood again.

The next day felt easier because she had so many excuses to avoid the viscount. The ladies had grown so bored with gossip and cards and staring out of the window bemoaning the fact it was winter that they decided to risk an excursion after all. Once they reluctantly decided Tunbridge Wells was too far to go on a short January day, she was kept busy organising a trip to Canterbury and making sure nobody got lost on the way there or back.

By the time they returned to Tolbourne House it was almost dark and the guests were fretful and weary after what was a strenuous day by their standards. They ate their dinner quietly and retired to their rooms soon after tea had been served to the ladies in the drawing room. If the gentlemen sat up over their brandy and tall tales it was not something a hostess needed to worry about. The footmen would get them upstairs to bed if they had overindulged and Martha could go to bed. When she got to her room she could congratulate herself on a whole day passing without her spending even a moment of it alone with Lord Elderwood, and that was much better, wasn't it?

Only three days to go now—two if she decided not to count Caro's supposed wedding day. Since Martha planned to be gone before that day dawned, she felt justified in striking that one off her list as well. Just two whole days left, and then there would be a tense wait for everyone to go to sleep before she and Noakes stole away into the night so neither of them would have to face the uproar when the wedding day dawned without a bride. Elderwood would survive with only a dent in his pride, she assured herself as she lay in bed with an image of him riding beside or ahead of the carriages today lodged in her mind. Of course, he was more vibrant and compelling than any other gentleman who had braved the elements today on the visit to Canterbury. He was still a stranger, she told herself as she fell asleep with a foolish smile on her face which it would be best not to remember the next morning.

The viscount could have spent the night with another woman, Martha argued with herself while

Noakes carried on with the elaborate business of turning her into a rich man's granddaughter and viscountess-in-waiting. Only today and tomorrow to get through, she reminded herself half an hour later. She stopped and blinked at the sight of Lord Elderwood sitting on the steps where she had sat on their first morning after the engagement ball.

'Good morning, my lord,' she greeted him as brightly as she could manage when she had been hoping she would be early enough to evade him again.

'Good morning, Lady Fetherall. My groom is trying to get a saddle on my horse. He told me to go away because Thor will only dance about and show off all the more if I try to help him.'

'I will ask Graves to have my mare saddled and perhaps I will see you later, then, Lord Elderwood,' she said stiffly, wondering how she could get Graves to take her riding on lanes a stranger to this area would never find without revealing the fact that she didn't know the way either.

'My man is a redoubtable horseman, my lady. I only left him to it so he can swear at the brute in peace,' he said as the sound of iron-shod hooves on the cobbled yard indicated the man had succeeded all too well. Graves was leading out Caro's precious mare as well, so Martha had run out of reasons not to ride out with Lord Elderwood instead of her sister's groom; after all, she was supposed to be engaged to the wretched man.

'What a fine animal,' she was forced to admit, and even had to smile at the stallion's antics as he arched his neck at Caro's mare and the mare flirted right back at him.

'He can be,' Thor's owner said, as if there were days when even he doubted it, but the pride in his steely blue eyes said he was lying.

'He will outpace my sweet girl in a few moments so you had better take him up on the downs and let him have his head,' she said, snatching at one last chance to avoid both the horse and his rider.

'No, he likes her too much to be so ungallant, and Frome took him for a ride yesterday while we were in Canterbury so some of the fidgets have been ridden out of him.'

No need to ask why the viscount took a hack yesterday when Thor would have stamped and bellowed challenges at every other male horse in the cavalcade even if they were gelded.

'You were very elusive yesterday, my lady,' Elderwood told her as they rode out of the yard together.

'I had a lot to do,' she said.

'As we are to marry in two days, maybe it's time we got to know one another a little better.'

'Or maybe we already know too much,' she said stiffly. After the other night she certainly knew more than she should about his wickedly will-sapping kisses.

'You are not the woman you appear to be on the surface though, are you?'

'I'm not a skein of wool waiting to be unravelled, Lord Elderwood. I am a mundane mixture of fears and hopes and dreams much like the next person.'

'You're about as complicated as a woman can get,' he argued with a thoughtful frown.

Martha's heart jolted with fear. She didn't want him to look any harder at her currently very complicated life. She didn't want him to think too hard about the differences between the woman he had pledged to marry and the one riding beside him now.

'Most women are more complex than most men think we are. Maybe I just seem unusual to you because I can afford to reveal my true nature now that you are safely on my grandfather's hook, my lord,' she made herself say distantly, hoping he would be so offended he would ride off in a huff.

'There's many a slip twixt cup and lip,' he told her, as if *he* might be the one to balk at this marriage instead of Caro. Was that what he had meant the other night when he suggested they didn't marry after all?

Martha longed for him to dig his aristocratic heels in and refuse to marry her sister. It felt dangerous to want him to do that, so much so that her fingers clenched on the reins and the mare danced as if she felt the tension in her rider and thought Thor was distraction enough. Martha held her breath, waiting for Elderwood to tell her he was about to ride back to London on his fine horse and not come back to marry her sister, who wasn't here for him to marry anyway!

'You must have agreed to marry me for a reason,' she prompted.

'Ah, yes,' he murmured almost to himself. 'The reason we are here… We mustn't forget that, must we?'

'No, probably not,' she said uncertainly. The very

thing she had wanted to know so badly suddenly seemed to loom too close for comfort.

'My reasons are private, Lady Fetherall,' he said, as stiff and distant again as he was on their first night here. 'As are yours for agreeing to wed me.'

'Oh, everyone knows what they are,' she said, feeling unaccountably hurt that he wouldn't confide in her. But this was supposed to be a marriage of convenience, so why would he? She could imagine Caro shuddering at the risks Martha was taking; she wasn't behaving much like the supposedly meek and obedient Lady Fetherall. 'You have a fine old title, Lord Elderwood, and I don't,' she said to remind him that Caro was supposed to be a determined husband hunter and he was well worth the chase.

'Your basic requirement of any man who asks for your hand?' he said as if the words tasted bitter.

'Yes,' she said flatly, and with that, the true chasm between Viscount Elderwood and Mrs Martha Lington had never felt wider.

'I never particularly wanted one, you know?' he said coolly. 'They are a mixed blessing at the best of times. I would have thought you had found that out for yourself by now.'

'Maybe I have, but my grandfather has not.'

'And you always do as he bids you.'

It wasn't a question and it stung. He was right about Caro, until very recently, but Tom would have laughed long and hard at the notion that Martha ever did what she was told without questioning it from every angle and coming to her own conclusions first.

'I was raised to be obedient,' she lied. He could hardly argue with her when his ring would flash on her finger like a malevolent demon's green eye again tonight, for the benefit of Tolbourne and his wealth-obsessed cronies.

'I hate to think how much it has cost you over the years to temper that fiery spirit of yours with fake obedience to your grandfather, Caroline,' he said too seriously for comfort.

She should be glad he had used Caro's given name instead of her title because it reminded her why she was here. She had been so tempted to tell him the truth, but that was still impossible. By the time it *was* possible, she would be long gone, and it hurt to even imagine what he would think of her when he found out what she'd done.

'The price was too high,' she said hollowly. Terror of her grandfather's fury if she dared argue had cost Caro more than any woman should have to pay.

'Yes, your compliance with his obsession with rank saw you married to Fetherall and to me this time.'

He looked as if he was feeling the wrongness of this marriage on her behalf as well as his own for the first time. Guilt racked her so hard she had to distract herself from it by soothing the mare as she jibbed and snorted. She could clearly tell her rider wasn't Caro.

'You are a fine catch, Lord Elderwood,' she made herself say blithely.

'Would that I were not, then, for both our sakes,'

he said with a frown. 'If only my father were still alive, I would be merely the Honourable Zachary Chilton, who might be viscount one day if he lived long enough but no point betting on him.'

Zachary—his name was Zachary! She sounded it in her head, gloated over the fact she could think of him as his true self from now on. She should make a frivolous comment, remind him he didn't want to share secrets with her, but she didn't.

'My father worked himself to death trying to win back all *his* late father had lost at the card tables,' he went on bitterly, 'and you and I would still be strangers if my damned grandfather had an ounce of shame in his careless soul, Lady Fetherall. I marvel that one man could lose so much without a single thought for his wife and son.'

It sounded as if Zachary had been betrayed by his grandfather every bit as badly as she and Caro had been by theirs, and it felt like another layer of understanding between them that she could not afford to enjoy. But still she didn't stop him with the kind of careless comment she ought to have ready.

'My father lost his life for that folly in the end, and he had completed but half of what he thought was his sacred duty. My grandmother's pride never recovered from what her husband did behind her back, you see, and my grandfather left her and my father with nothing but debts and empty pockets. That's worse than having nothing, Lady Fetherall. *Nothing* gives you a place to start, but debt has to be paid back before you can even reach the heady heights of having nothing.'

'You don't appear to have *nothing* now,' she said with a glance at his fine stallion and elegant riding clothes.

'Because my father was a driven man—or should that be *a driven boy*, since he was little more than a boy when he inherited his father's lands and titles dragged down by mortgages and debts. He was determined not to wallow in a debtors' prison with no chance of being able to get out again so he bargained with his creditors, pawned the family jewels, worked the land back into profit, played the markets and robbed Peter to pay Paul. By the time he was forty he had paid off all the mortgages and Flaxonby—our ancestral home—was safe, but he was so worn out by the effort that he caught a stupid childhood fever from one of us and died not long afterwards. He was so determined to make sure I would inherit not a single unpaid debt from him, that I would never need to worry about money as he had, but now my little brother and youngest sister barely remember him.'

He paused and seemed to remember where he was and whom he was talking to. 'Still, at least you will never need worry that I can't keep you in the style to which you are accustomed, my lady. We Chiltons have come a long way since my wastrel grandfather died, and I certainly don't need your grandfather's money.'

Of course she wouldn't, but she wasn't Caro. Martha felt even more sure she and Caro were doing the right thing because facing a loveless marriage and a family determined to reject her would have hurt her sister deeply; Caro was so hungry for love that it would be unbearable for her to be kept on the outside of a close family for ever. Martha could only imagine the penny pinching and pride it had taken to dig the Chilton family out of the mire in which Zachary's grandfather had sunk them, but their struggle only made them seem even further out of Caro and Martha's orbit than before she knew about it. They had clung on to their noble heritage against the odds, dragged themselves out of beggary, and could now hold their heads up high again.

She thought of her Winton grandparents' pride in their ancient manor, and in the remote and often harsh lands they called home, and in their eternal struggle to keep it all going and making a good enough living for the family, the tenants and all the estate workers. Her grandparents had a lot in common with the viscount, even if their lives were lived on a smaller scale. But what did he have in common with her? She was an unacknowledged Tolbourne after all, a rejected child, labelled a bastard.

Not that it mattered, she reminded herself glumly, since Zachary Chilton wouldn't be marrying her the day after tomorrow.

Chapter Six

'What *do* you need so badly that you agreed to marry me, then?' Martha asked him bluntly, because she needed to know now, and not for Caro's sake but her own. She had thought such hard things about him before she came here and now it looked as if he had been driven into this marriage as surely as Caro had been.

'My late grandmother was a great heiress,' he said stiffly, as if he didn't want to say more but perhaps his bride-to-be deserved an explanation.

Martha felt another stab of guilt because she wasn't that bride at all, but she still wanted to know why he agreed to marry Caro so she said nothing.

'She was the last of a great family, Lady Fetherall, heiress to all they had built up over centuries. She even insisted on styling herself the Lady Margaret DeMayne-Chilton, Viscountess Elderwood, when she married my grandfather to preserve her family name. Then he killed himself rather than face what he had done, and once he was gone she found out he had lost everything she had inherited and a lot more besides. She had to hide from the duns and count every crust of bread she put in her children's mouths.'

'It must have been very hard for her,' Martha said carefully because she thought Lady Margaret sounded very proud and haughty and she would have been horrified that her grandson had lowered himself to marry a Tolbourne.

'I don't remember her smiling even once,' Zachary said as if he thought he had to explain the effect of his grandmother's bitter losses to the pampered granddaughter of a cit with no proud heritage to lose. 'She was the most feted heiress of her generation, bringing to her marriage Holdfast Castle and all the wild border land her forefathers had held for the English king. Her feckless husband lost every penny and every stick and stone of it. Then he went back to the card tables and lost everything else he could lay his hands on until there was nothing left and finally the coward shot himself.'

'For her to have faced such a terrible loss and not collapse under it must have taken a lot of courage,' Martha said carefully. She was still puzzled as to why he must marry Caro when his father had redeemed the mortgages and made sure his son would inherit Flaxonby Hall and his extensive estate free of debt.

'Aye, she was a formidable woman,' Zachary said as if he had very mixed feelings about his steely grandmother. 'Obsessive and driven and proud as the devil, but she was brave and admirable as well, in her own way.'

'Was she very difficult to live with?'

'Very,' he said with a rueful shrug then a wry smile at her for guessing how it must have felt to live with such a demanding and embittered woman. 'You are a lot shrewder than you pretend to be, aren't you, my lady?'

'It would be hard for me to be less so than I pretend to be, wouldn't it?'

He gave her a long, coolly assessing look and Martha felt her hands sweating inside Caro's supple riding gloves. She cursed herself for being such a fool as to draw his attention to the gap between her appearance and her true character.

'Indeed,' he said, 'it is a very good act.'

'We all act a part in our own way, though, don't we?'

'Maybe,' he conceded and for a while there was only the sound of their horses' hooves and the jingle of Thor's bridle as he shook his head and snorted at Caro's mare to remind her how restless and untamed he could be when he wasn't pretending to be a tame hack for her sake.

'How old were you when Lady Margaret died?' she asked to try to divert his attention back onto his grandmother.

'Fourteen,' he said as if he were remembering being the bewildered and fatherless youth who had been forced to face another loss, but as the head of the family that time. Caro had told her that Viscount Elderwood had inherited his title at the age of twelve. Martha imagined the grieving boy he must have been trying to match up to his haughty grandmother's stern expectation that he take his father's place, when he was far too young to be anything more than a schoolboy who needed to grow up first.

'She used to watch me like a hawk for the slightest sign that I had inherited any of my grandfather's weakness and before she died she made me promise I would get her all of her own grand heritage back in the family one day. My father believed it was his duty to regain everything of hers his father had lost so I would have done so anyway, even without the vow,' he told her.

Martha hated the idea of his grandparents ruling his life from beyond the grave as Tolbourne tried to rule Caro's. It sounded like Zachary had been trapped by old sins, and not all of them were his grandfather's.

Poor little boy, she thought but dare not say to the strong man he was now. She suddenly realised why the name Holdfast sounded familiar. Caro had mentioned the place Tolbourne had in the north because she used to hope her grandfather would visit it and she would be able to sneak over to Greygil for furtive visits to her sister, but he never went there. Apparently he had told his agent to squeeze every penny out of the musty old place and not bother him with petty details; that sounded like very rough possession to her.

'Holdfast Castle,' she said flatly.

'Indeed,' Zachary said as if he had been waiting for her to make the connection.

'It can't be worth a great deal if my s—' she said clumsily and nearly gave the game away before Caro was safe! How stupid and unwary! Her heart was now racing for a very different reason than her constant awareness of this man who clearly wanted Holdfast Castle back very badly. 'My grandfather will have wrung it dry without spending a farthing on it so it won't be a great prize anymore, I fear. And before you accuse me of wilful ignorance, I know that's what he does,' she managed to say stiffly. She hoped he was too furious about Tolbourne's business methods to recall that she had begun to say something different. 'I dare say you could buy it cheaply enough, if you feel you must,' she added for good measure.

'I would, if only he would sell it to me. I must have seemed too eager when I approached him with an offer to buy it a couple of years ago. I had inherited full control of my fortune and could spend my father's hard-earned wealth on his dearest dream, but your grandfather refused to sell it to me.'

'He made it my marriage portion, didn't he?' she said as the pieces finally dropped into place. How she hated the shape of them. 'That's why you agreed to marry me, isn't it?'

Tolbourne had trapped the viscount through that promise to his grandmother, a promise Zachary would consider sacred, and through the guilt his father felt at the loss of his mother's grand inheritance. If he married Caro he would regain Holdfast and be able to put *his* grandfather's last unpaid debt to bed. Now, because of her interference, the castle and all it must have come to represent when his father died so tragically young would slip through Zachary's fingers. What fresh horror was this? She felt as if she had robbed him of something so important that he would never forgive her, not when he knew what she and her sister had done.

'I feel sick,' she said numbly.

'It's not your fault, Caroline,' Zachary said. Maybe he was right; it wasn't Caro's fault, but it could easily be hers.

'You don't know that,' she said with an agitated wave at the hills between here and Tolbourne House because she couldn't look Zachary in the eye knowing what she had done to him. 'You have no idea,' she added and wondered if she should confess the truth and risk her sister's happiness after all.

No, there could still be time for a very determined gentleman to ride that mighty stallion all the way to Gretna and stop Caro escaping this misbegotten marriage. Caro had to have her chance at happiness at last. Her half-sister had been forced to waste so much of her young life on Tolbourne's proud folly and now she was with child. Martha knew that Caro deserved every mile she could get between here and Gretna.

So, Martha must keep being Caroline, Lady Fetherall, for every moment she could manage it until the day of her supposed wedding to Zachary,

Lord Elderwood. Even though it meant grinding his plans and dreams into dust.

'Did you arrange this marriage, Caroline? Did you write this farce we are both being forced to play?' Zachary demanded as if he were thoroughly exasperated with her melodramatic response.

'Of course I didn't, but I could have been stronger. I should have refused to come back here and do as he bid me when my husband died.'

Oh, confound it, but now she was falling ever deeper into a mire of her own making. She was saying what Caro had been too frightened to when this engagement was forced on her. Her lies seemed more twisted by the moment but she had to carry on telling them; there was no way out of this mess but to go on with it despite now feeling sick with guilt about Zachary's coming disappointment, as well as ridiculously attracted to him. That only proved what a fool she was.

'Easy to say but hard to do,' he said gently, as if he understood how appalling her sister's life had been under first Tolbourne's control and then Fetherall's.

Martha's guilt felt solid as a lump of lead in her belly as she stared into the distance trying to pretend nothing had changed now that she knew the truth behind the hollow marriage Caro was so desperate not to make.

'You understand too much, Zachary. It is more than I deserve,' she said carefully at last. It was the first time she had called him by his first name and it felt important.

'I have been a child trying to live a grown-up life too, Caroline—if you were ever allowed to be a child in the first place, and you were certainly no more than one when you married Fetherall. Perhaps we have more in common than we thought possible at the start of our engagement.'

Ah, yes, our engagement. Don't forget about that, Martha. 'I can't see many similarities myself,' she made herself say lightly.

'But we have a common future.'

She could have sworn he hadn't wanted one when he had stood at the bottom of the stairs a few days ago glaring up at her like a trapped beast. Now he was trying to say he might have learned to want it after all, but he was only making the best of a bad lot. It would feel even more wrong for her to sit here pretending to be Caro as their horses walked placidly side by side if he really meant that he now saw their marriage as something he might actually want for more than just the sake of the castle.

'Because of an old promise you made your grandmother and a duty you feel towards your father,' she argued.

She stared between the mare's ears so she didn't have to look at him, so she didn't long for this lie to be true. Was she really so stupid with wanting him that she would be willing to exchange her life for Caro's if she could, if it meant she ended up married to Zachary, Viscount Elderwood? No, even Martha Lington wasn't that deluded. The wanting would pass soon enough when she wasn't seeing him every day.

'There was more than that between us the other night,' he reminded her as if it was his trump card.

'Yes, there was lust and two people young enough and curious enough to make mischief in the dark together,' she said bleakly. Martha wished she could go now, before this ache settled into her heart and forced her to face things she didn't want to admit to herself and to this viscount she had come here to deceive.

Luckily Thor grew tired of pretending to be a quiet and gentlemanly horse at just the right moment so Zachary could not respond to her comment about the kiss being a quick fumble in the dark. The stallion began to prance and even tried to rear as if he wanted to show off his power and princely spirit to the indifferent mare. It was the perfect excuse for Martha to tell Zachary to go and gallop the fidgets out of him while she trotted the mare back to Tolbourne House; she used the excuse of wanting to be back and changed in good time to play hostess to her grandfather's guests.

The routine of consulting the cook about the fussier guests' preferences and resolving any dilemmas the housekeeper felt were beyond her remit and reminded Martha that Caro was far more capable and organised than most people gave her credit for. Caro would soon have a house of her own to run and Martha thought she would be very happy as the beloved wife of a comfortably off country gentleman. Mr Harmsley would certainly never have any cause to

complain about her sister's housekeeping—not that
he seemed likely to.

Martha allowed herself a smile for those two and
fervently hoped they were already across the border
and married. She felt a little better about deceiving
Zachary because as she saw it, it was either her sister's happiness or his. However bad a lie this was, it
was the only way to make sure Caro and Harmsley
ended up married to one another instead of mired in
the appalling mess it would have been if the pregnant
Caro had been forced to marry Zachary.

Despite the brief lifting of her spirits at the thought
that at least Caro and Harmsley would be blissfully
happy if this deception worked, Martha spent the
rest of the day battling with her conscience and woke
up the next morning to do it again. The very idea of
Zachary waiting at the altar for a bride who never
came had always felt too much of a humiliation to
want to inflict on him, but now she knew him and his
motives for marrying Caro it was unthinkable. She
had managed to avoid being alone with him again
for the rest of yesterday and most of today, but she
found she missed his company sorely.

Now it was the eve of what should have been
Caro's wedding day and Martha was so confused by
her feelings towards the about-to-be-frustrated groom
that she kept him at arm's length all evening in case
she could not control her tongue. If she was going
to dash Zachary's hopes of getting his hands on his
grandmother's castle, then at least Caro and Harmsley must get the future together that they deserved.

This was only ever meant to be a week's charade. She was the wrong woman in the right place and nobody was supposed to get hurt. Yet her conflicted feelings about Zachary's quest to regain his family honour made her question so much about her own life and choices as well as her half-sister's. She had too much time to think this evening as she tried to keep Tolbourne's restless and bored guests amused one last time. She was torn between furtively trying to stamp Zachary's image on her memory and trying to start forgetting him.

She had pretended she was happy working with Grandfather Winton on the farm for the last five years since Tom died, and she had certainly been busy enough to forget she wasn't most of the time. She had worked with her grandfather to improve the flocks for the benefit of all the families that depended on them for their livelihood. It had felt better to slip back into a way of life that demanded so much from her that she was able to sleep soundly at the end of each day and wake with the dawn eager to start again. Driving herself so hard meant she could block out her pain at missing Tom, but it had also meant that she wasn't really living, or feeling, or even thinking very much. Maybe she needed to stop and examine what she was doing to herself by isolating herself at Greygil and refusing to find time to socialise with their neighbours.

Now she had to put all her effort into avoiding Zachary instead of into burying her grief for her late husband. She already missed his sharp interest in the world around him and his quick understanding, and these feelings made Tom seem less vivid than he ever had before. It felt so strange when Tom had played such a large part in her childhood as well as being the love of her young life. It felt disloyal of her to be lonely for another man. She found it a little too easy to drift off into a dream world, to let herself think of a life she could have been about to start with Zachary, if he had needed to marry *her* in the morning and not Caro.

It wouldn't have been any better than the marriage he came here to make with her sister. It would have been far worse in fact, because Martha could have fallen in love with the man and that would have led to misery not bliss. She wasn't even going to think about her nights which were now haunted by fantasies of having Zachary as her rampant and fascinated lover instead of Tom. How could she long for him when she had loved her husband so very much and lived for every second that he was home on leave?

Zachary had only kissed her that night because he was trying to find out if he could forge some common ground with the woman he had to marry in order to stay true to a promise he had made his father and grandmother. He could only have been so passionate about it because of Caro's low-cut gowns and because he had been thinking about finally getting back the castle he cared so deeply about. A good man lived behind Viscount Elderwood's sternly handsome Viking looks and sometimes arrogant manner. She almost smiled at the thought of him feeling so frustrated by this week of waiting to marry Lady Fetherall that he had even risked kissing her in the dark to find out if they might make a go of that marriage against the odds.

Now Martha felt edgy and weary instead of excited at the prospect of being liberated from her lies and this horrible, overdecorated house. She had longed for this week to be over all the time she and Caro were planning it. Now it was bedtime on the last day she would ever have to spend here and she refused to be wistful about the routines of this place that might as well have been Caro's prison.

She risked a sideways glance at Zachary and realised this was the last time she would ever set eyes on him. He looked very serious and must have been trying to gauge how she really felt about this being the eve of their wedding because he met her gaze with a questioning look that said he saw beneath the paint on her face and the scantily cut deep gold satin gown to the troubled thoughts beneath. The gown had been intended to show Lady Fetherall anticipating a triumphant wedding day—at least according to Noakes, who had taken one look at Martha's tired eyes and preoccupied frown this afternoon and ordered her to lie down with pads soaked in something cool and soothing on her eyes for half an hour.

'Goodnight, my lord,' she said to Zachary, and willed her hand not to shake as he took it and pressed a kiss on the back of it as if he meant it.

'Goodnight, my lady,' he said as if he were looking forward to her being his wife tomorrow night.

She reminded herself how revolted he had looked when he took her hand that first night to lead her into the ballroom and refused to meet his eyes again. 'Sweet dreams,' she heard him murmur as she took her candle.

Hot wax dripped on her hand as the notion that he might suspect how heavily he had featured in her dreams ever since the night they had met shook her. She gasped at the shock of it but he had already reached her side to brush away the congealed wax and gaze down at the slight redness it had left on her wrist. The sting was already fading, but he raised her wrist to his face as if he needed to see it wasn't serious while she held her breath like an unfledged girl as this man who would never be hers kissed her wrist in full view of anyone who was watching.

'To kiss it better,' he told her and grinned like a schoolboy when she could find no words to say it already was.

Feeling like a blushing schoolgirl when he let her go, she hid that hand in her slippery gold skirts. At least they were a good reminder she was supposed to be a woman of the world.

'Until tomorrow,' she made herself say lightly and went upstairs without looking back.

Chapter Seven

'Well, it's done, then,' Noakes said when Martha hurried into Caro's room and shut the door behind her. She leaned against it for a moment while she got her racing heart under control.

Martha took a steadying breath and tried not to feel the memory of Zachary's last kiss on her wrist. 'Yes, all done,' she said brightly.

'Your valise is packed and I managed to put us both a bundle of food together for the first day or so.'

'You know how to get back to London or to wherever Caro is going after the wedding?'

'Aye, I'm going to—'

'No, don't tell me, for then I can't give them away if Tolbourne does manage to find me despite all my efforts to keep him off my tail. You had better slip outside before the butler locks all the doors.'

'Best we don't leave together. I've put a key to the garden door in your reticule and everyone's worn out by the fuss over the wedding. The staff will soon be fast asleep even if the guests take longer to settle.'

'It's all right, Noakes, you can stop fussing. I will give them time to settle and change out of Caro's finery before I go, I promise. I'm a big girl now.'

'Are you sure you don't want me to help you undress?'

'No, just go before it's too late to sneak out without us both having to wait a couple of hours until it's safe to leave. You know we stand more chance of getting away if you slip out now. We both know one or two servants do it every night and you know how to cover your tracks.'

'As if I'd do something like that!' Noakes said with an outraged sniff, then shocked Martha by giving her a hug and telling her she was a good girl before she went.

'Am I, Noakes, am I really?' Martha whispered to herself as she stood in the midst of all this gilded splendour in her silly gold gown. She didn't feel in the least bit good.

Viscount Elderwood was nothing like the entitled idiot Martha had expected to meet when she went downstairs that first night to face his compelling silver-blue gaze with a fast-beating heart. She knew she owed him her relative freedom these last few days after he made even Tolbourne respect him and keep his cronies from ogling her. For that alone Zachary didn't deserve a humiliating wait at the altar for a bride who had never intended to marry him in the first place.

Now she had done all she could for Caro and

Harmsley, she owed it to Zachary to let him know that she wasn't going to marry him tomorrow. No need for her to explain why—he would find that out soon enough—but she would rather he hated Martha Lington at a distance while he was doing so. When news of Caro and Harmsley's elopement came out, everyone would know the woman posing as Lady Fetherall this week has been an imposter, but by then Martha would be long gone. She still flinched at the thought of Zachary's fury when he found out he had been tricked, and that he wouldn't be getting his grandmother's castle back. She couldn't allow him to wait at the altar for a bride who was probably already married to another man by now. She had to tell him she could not be his inconvenient bride, even if he brought all his fury to bear on her for what she had done.

'Caroline…' Zach couldn't call her Lady Fetherall tonight somehow.

'Zachary…' she replied with a brief smile that did something dangerous to his insides. He wondered why she looked so nervous while she made a half-hearted attempt to tease him for his hesitation over her name. He hadn't realised he didn't want to call her by that lout Fetherall's title ever again, and at least tomorrow they would finally be rid of it.

'You shouldn't have come,' he murmured with a hasty look down the corridor to make sure nobody else was about.

'I had to. Are you going to let me in?' she said urgently, and something told him she had not come to say *And let's anticipate our wedding night.*

'Since we are to wed tomorrow, I expect it's almost allowed,' he said ruefully and stood back to let her walk into his room. He suspected she was very pale under her usual paint and yet she looked oddly resolute, as if she had come to do or say something she didn't want to, but it still had to be said.

'That's why I'm here,' she said and confirmed his worst suspicions.

'Good,' he said and kissed her because he didn't want to hear her say whatever it was she had come here to tell him.

He carried on doing it because he liked kissing her so much and it seemed a shame to stop. The softness of her surprised mouth under his felt deliciously familiar. He remembered how sweet her response had been last time he kissed her but this was even better, far more intimate now they could be assured of privacy and she had walked into his den of her own accord.

He felt fire flash between them and thought that the roar of mutual desire would soon make her forget what she was here to tell him, or at least he hoped so. It felt as if this was his reward for being such a good, patient viscount for almost a week. He wasn't even going to think about how stiff and impatient he had intended to remain towards her. Desire roared through him fiercer than he could ever remember it when she opened her mouth to let his tongue in, as if she couldn't help herself either, and she tangled hers with his on a wordless groan that did terrible things to his fabled self-control.

He adored this feeling of total intimacy as her tongue met with his, as her breath mingled with his until he could hardly tell which of them had to pant the hardest to wrench air into their protesting lungs so they could keep on exploring and enticing and inciting one another to more. It was the best sort of communication between a passionate man and a passionate woman and the only sort he wanted right now. He didn't want to hear what she had come to tell him. He had this contradictory, fiery and usually guarded woman in his arms, and she was kissing him back as if her last breath depended on him so he certainly wasn't going to waste any of his breath asking why.

He had already done his masculine duty of checking that this was a safe place for them to forget the rest of the world, so he put all his energies back into seducing her. Since he was going to marry her tomorrow, why not?

Martha felt all the reasons why this was impossible slip away. None of them seemed to matter when he was kissing her so ardently, and she had forgotten what they were. She gave up even trying to list why this was a terrible idea and decided to simply enjoy the moment as if that was all that was important. She let his desire and all this fire and sheer need between them push aside the fraud she was perpetrating on him; she needed him so very badly that it almost hurt. She felt the sheer physical pleasure of being this close to a man who was so warm and urgent and, oh, so delightfully human. His mouth feasted on hers and his tongue told her erotic stories of all the intimate things he wanted to do with her. Hers said she wanted him to and please would he make her forget who she was for a glorious, forbidden moment and never mind tomorrow?

It's been so long, the weak little excuse echoed round her mind and she knew it wasn't enough to explain this joyous abandon. She let the heat and strength of him drown out the stern inner voice that wanted to argue there was no comparison. She had loved Tom Lington, had known him better than she knew herself, had laughed with him, had almost been part of him ever since she ended up at Greygil and he lived in the next valley. Tom had been almost as familiar to her as her own face in the mirror and far, far dearer. She didn't want to admit it as she fought for a bit of rational space in her overheated brain, but even Tom had never kissed her as deeply and passionately as Zachary was now. He hadn't wanted her as overwhelmingly as she could feel lordly Zachary Chilton wanting her either, and by making her want him back so urgently she felt even more wicked than she was already. Even without the viscount's insistent manhood so hard against her body, despite his gentlemanly breeches and her fine petticoat, she would have known how desperate he was for the ultimate intimacy because his mouth was telling her he was, and so was his tongue via the few whispered words he could spare from kissing her as if his life depended on it. Now his hands were urgent on her neat derriere, and he pulled her even further against the arousal they had both been fighting so hard for nearly a week.

No, don't think about how short a time you will know him, Martha—just seize the day for once and snatch pleasure before this charade falls apart.

He used his strength to let her know he was desperate for her, and she wondered what it would be like were he to unleash it. Then there was that inner poet she had once speculated about whispering soft seduction against her skin and expressing all the needs and desires she'd thought she would never experience again in what felt like an unstoppable tide. If he was at the very edge of reason and about to dive right in to rash, unreasoning passion with her, then she wanted him every bit as passionately. She could be afraid of so much raw male power held on such a thin leash but instead she loved it. All she dreaded right now was feeling him pull back from their ultimate completion, deciding the right thing to do would be to postpone the frantic ending to this heat and sensuality for a wedding night she knew was never going to happen. She did her best to make him forget such nonsense with a long moan of need and demand that broke that leash with a deeply satisfying snap.

It felt glorious as his touch deepened on her wanting body. She felt as if time had stalled so they could have as much of it as they needed to make this moment perfect. She felt Zach's fingers suddenly clumsy as he fumbled with the laces of her gown and then lose patience with them. She managed a low hum of approval when she heard and felt Caro's flimsy gown give in as those laces were ripped out of their holes. Neither Tolbourne sister would ever have to wear such a travesty of a gown again and it felt liberating and exciting to watch the shreds of this very expensive satin gown gliding to the floor like feathers even as Zachary eyed the imprisoning, provoking, overenthusiastic corset beneath it with a disapproving frown.

Impatient with it as well, she snatched at the bow that tied its laces so tight and felt the easing of the pressure it had always put on her body with a sigh of relief. She felt powerful and shameless as cool air kissed her breasts. They peaked under the viscount's avid gaze and his once icy blue eyes went molten.

Both of them attacked the pushing, confining thing they couldn't get undone fast enough. Laces flew out of more eyelet holes and the dratted thing finally loosened its grip on her torso and she could breathe freely again. It felt as if it was a symbol of all that the Tolbourne sisters would be free of from this moment on, a triumph for both of them when the cramping, humiliating thing finally gave up its tight hold on her body and Zachary threw it across the room as if he despised it as much as she did.

Her chemise was soon just one more sliver of torn silk he tore off her with such haste that she had no idea where that unmourned piece of Lady Fetherall's disguise went either. Now she was naked but for her stockings and Caro's kid slippers. They had always pinched so Martha kicked them off as well.

'What about you?' she asked as Zachary eyed her bare body as if he had been starving for the sight of her this way all week. She wanted him to feast on her so very badly that it felt like a force of nature inside her, a need that was going to plague her for the rest of her life without him. But she wasn't going to think about that while she was busily wringing every ounce of pleasure she could out of what was going to be their one and only time together.

'You are still very clothed indeed, my lord viscount,' she said with a speculative gaze at his beautifully cut evening coat and all the accoutrements of a very fine gentleman he must be wearing underneath it.

'As you are not, my lady,' he said huskily. He eyed her stockings so speculatively that she was certain her garters would have gone the same way as the rest of her sister's fine clothes if she hadn't dodged his reaching hands with a smile and shake of the head that made the pins in her already tousled hair fall out and her long curls kiss her naked back.

'Yet here I am all unguarded and naked while you have kept all your clothes on. You do know that's not fair, don't you, Zachary?'

'Ah, but you're so much more worth looking at than I am.'

'I'll be the judge of that,' she said and dodged another move to lift her into his arms and onto his bed as his ice blue eyes ate her up from a distance. She felt her nipples tighten and her stomach flip as if she was about to jump from a great height—and maybe she was. She was still determined to take him with her when she went but not quite yet. 'Strip, my lord,' she ordered him, with her hands guarding her secret inner self from his gaze to even up the odds a little.

He must have heard the husk of all she wanted to do with him in her voice because even as he shook his head and stared reproachfully at her guarding hands, his own were busy tugging at his elegantly tied cravat as if it felt too tight around his strong and surprisingly tanned neck so he might as well be rid of it. His coat went next and what a good thing his tailor wasn't here to see how little respect His Lordship had for his artistry as it flew across the room to join her scattered garments. She giggled at the thought of their expensive clothes sympathising with each other in the dark after such rough treatment, and they were of such exquisite quality you would have thought their wearers should know that they deserved better.

'What's so funny?' he asked gruffly, as if he thought it might be the sight of him hastily shucking off his lordly elegance under her fascinated gaze.

'All the layers of finery we wrap ourselves in so you can't see me like this and I don't have to imagine what you look like without yours for much longer.'

'You talk too much,' he told her and the glitter in his fascinating eyes told her he was beyond teasing and almost beyond words.

'Then hurry,' she told him and at last his myriad of waistcoat buttons gave in to his rough handling and he stripped that garment off with an impatient sigh.

His shirt took so much untucking and unlacing and throwing off that she wanted to go and help him, but if she did she knew he would seize her and she would lose her chance to watch him naked and strong and vulnerable at the same time. He would not be able to hide an iota of his need from her when they were naked.

Ah, there was his chest exposed and even harder with muscle and more powerful than she had imagined it in her wildest dreams. Then his shoulders were gloriously naked as he shucked off his polite gentleman's undershirt as well. It was evident he was no layabout as he was golden skinned and sleekly muscular—perhaps he actually worked with his men in the fields at harvest time, she thought. The prospect made her like him all the more. She avoided his next attempt to grab her and gestured that there was more to go before they were truly equal since she couldn't speak for wanting him.

She still wanted a private view of those intriguing parts of himself that Lord Elderwood kept hidden from all but the most privileged of her sex, so she refused to let this ache and need and tenderness rob her of it and give in too quickly to her own fiery demand for completion. This was the image of him she would have to hold in her heart for the rest of her life so she needed to treasure tonight in her secret fantasies. She knew he would refuse to have any more to do with such a liar when he found out what she had done, so this was the first and last time they would ever make love. At least this way she could have the memory of him magnificently, unmistakably, rigidly aroused to keep her warm even when he hated her from afar.

She gazed at him even more hungrily as she tried to imprint every last detail on her memory and held her breath as he undid the flap of his breeches at long last. But then he had to bend down to undo the buckles at his knees before he could strip them off. How much more convenient it would be if gentlemen wore pantaloons rather than keeping a lover waiting impatiently for the rest of their finery to be gone of an evening. Except his breeches and silk stockings did show off his fine manly legs to perfection, she decided, as he managed to remove them in record time, and even then his cotton underdrawers hid his straining manhood from her eager eyes.

She shook her head and waved a provocative hand at her own naked body to say she had nothing left to hide behind and neither should he. It was a wonder to her that she didn't feel in the least bit self-conscious with him. She felt free and powerful like a true siren as colour burned high on his cheeks. He gazed at her as if he wanted to dive right into their mutual pleasure, and whatever were they waiting for?

Then he wasn't wearing anything and she had been so fascinated by his hot ice blue gaze that she didn't even see his last move to remove all traces of clothing as her borrowed garters finally flew into that dark corner of the room and would never be any use again. She eyed his lordly, rigid manhood with awe and a certain amount of trepidation because she could see that he really did want her mightily and it had been so long since she'd had a lover in her bed, let alone one so rampant.

'See,' he said in such a scraped-raw voice that she knew he was almost beyond speech again.

This delicious spectacle must end any moment now, but she *did* see and she felt the pull of extreme need snag mercilessly at her feminine core now that she could finally see him in all his naked glory. She saw the clean lines of his long muscular legs and narrow hips and that every inch of him was tense with wanting her. He was watching her as if he thought she might be shocked by so much of him so desperate for her. Bless the man, but he was nervous!

As if she might want to pick out some tiny fault and reject him! Had he never exposed himself to anyone quite this openly before? Not that she thought he usually made love with his shirt on, or avoided being naked with his mistress, but whatever had passed between them this week had stripped away the debonair viscount and put Zachary the man fully on display as he would never have allowed himself to be before. There was something touching about his waiting nakedness, as if he was silently telling her that he knew the truth of her too and now they were equal.

Except it wasn't the truth. She was Martha, the

needy liar, who was going to blow his dreams apart. She ought to grab a sheet and run out of the room but she didn't have the strength to turn her back on loving this man to the heights and depths just once before he hated her for making a fool of him.

His complicated gaze was wary as well as avid as he took in every curve of her body in the fire-light. Did he think she was intimidated by his huge need and might turn away with a polite *No, thank you*? Idiot man if that was why he hadn't breached the distance between them yet. She told him so with eager eyes and flushed cheeks and made herself meet his eyes with everything she wanted and needed in her own. Surely he could tell how desperately she wanted him just from the look of her parted lips and her nipples were so tight they hurt for the lack of his touch? She was hardly in a position to hide any of it and he must know enough about women to realise she was beyond desperate for him, for his hugely aroused manhood and for his ravenous mouth and urgent touch.

Chapter Eight

Zach felt as if they had peeled off all the layers of self-protection that even lovers usually kept up between them. For a long moment, as she gazed at him with wide, dazed eyes, he was tempted to do as Adam did after the fall and cover himself with his hands then see if he could find some fig leaves to hide his mercilessly hard and urgent arousal. Except her eyes held his eagerly as if she never wanted to look away again, and suddenly he felt no shame at all, only need and intimacy and a deep trust he had never managed to find with any of his lovers before her. Who would have thought at the beginning of all this that Lady Fetherall would turn out to be someone so special, when he'd been manoeuvred into marrying her very much against his will?

With a fierce shake of his head, he forced aside an uneasy memory of his plan not to touch her, and to divorce her as soon as she took a lover. He saw uncertainty in her eyes, a shake in her hand where it covered her sex from his gaze, as if she felt the need to hide that last and very private part of herself from him even now.

'No, that's not what I meant,' he explained huskily. He didn't want to let even the thought of her grandfather or his into the room to remind them of who they were with their clothes on, so he told her the truth instead. 'I want you too much,' he admitted gruffly. 'I need you too much,' he added and saw her eye his rigidly erect sex with awe before she smiled rather smugly, as if she was proud of being able to arouse him so visibly, so rampantly.

How the hell was he going to be gentle with her when she gave such admiring looks to his grinding, merciless need? Somehow he had to control himself while he made this good for her before he could ride her up to the stars and—and never mind all the rest of the things he wanted to do to her right now. If he thought about that he was going to disgrace himself before he had even laid a hand on her naked body. He frowned at the marks the corset had left on her skin and soothed one with his index finger, exploring the harsh and reddened lines that the damned thing had left on her creamy skin, and finding enough gentleness in himself after all.

'Promise me you will never let one of those things bite into you like this ever again. I don't need to be told how glorious your figure is under the silk and satins, my lady, because now I know it for certain,' he told her, and tenderness outdid even his raging need for satisfaction so he was confident he would be able to control himself when the time came. He could gentle himself for her, for as long as it took her to trust him with everything she was and would be after they were married. They could move on to frantic lovemaking when she was confident enough to be with him all the way.

Martha almost told him she wasn't who he thought she was when he stared at her with such tender, wanting eyes. She felt guilt threaten to cool a little of her ardour even as she knew she wasn't going to tell him anything that would make him flinch away from her and put his clothes back on. He wanted to be a kind and considerate lover to his future wife when all Martha wanted was his haste and need and the delicious, delirious satisfaction she knew he was going to give her as soon as she could persuade him that she wanted this every bit as much as he did.

She didn't have the memories of abuse and drunken insults or any of the other humiliations her sister would have were she here instead. Martha had only ever been loved with respect and tenderness by her late and truly gentle husband and best friend. Right now she wanted Zachary's outright, blazing passion since it was going to have to burn hot enough to keep her warm for the rest of her life. She never thought she could want another man after Tom died but how wrong she had been. It had been so long since she had been loved deeply and surely, but she would have time to feel guilty about it later—when she was brutally alone with the memory of this man's passion for the woman he thought she was, before he found out she wasn't Caro.

She eyed him with a hot, speculative sort of wonder again and knew she had to override his noble resolution to be infinitely gentle with the abused woman she realised he suspected Caro would have been, if they had ever got this close. Martha had never truly been jealous of Caro before, but she was now. She blotted out that uncomfortable truth because tonight *she* would be Zachary's lover and that was what mattered.

'I never want to wear such a monstrosity again. I want to breathe and live and move freely. I want to do all the things Lady Fetherall never could. I want to ride until dusk with you and run down hillsides to roll in the wet grass and dance at sunrise, Zachary. I want to do all that without you wondering if I'm too fragile, or hurt, or delicate to do it without breaking. I want it all, but mostly I want you.' Every word was true in the moment, but it was only a delightful fantasy since she would not be walking up the aisle to marry him tomorrow.

'You are so brave,' he told her as he stepped forward and cupped her chin so she had to look him fully in the eyes and yet not let him see too much.

'I'm the biggest coward in Christendom,' she argued huskily and was too enthralled to look away.

'No, if I say you're brave, don't argue.'

'I won't, my lord,' she said and danced wickedly knowing fingers down his impressively muscled chest and around his tight masculine nipples. He gasped and she watched them harden with a low feminine growl of approval.

Excellent, she gloated as she let her grazing touch glide on to appreciate the tight, tense bands of muscle across his belly. He wanted her so much that she had to break his rigid self-control soon or else she would burst into flames from the inside out. She let her butterfly caress flit to his rigid manhood and felt every sense and cell of him tighten.

'I promise not to argue with this part of you, my lord,' she teased, and wondered if it was a mistake when he went still as a statue under her touch. He might have enough iron determination to push her back into some clothes and out of his room before he disgraced himself, as he thought, with a fragile woman. Except she wasn't fragile; she was lusty and eager and hot frustration was burning deep inside her and screaming for more.

'I need you as a desert needs rain,' she leaned up to whisper in his ear, brushing her rigidly wanting nipples against him as she rubbed her aching breasts against his torso. 'I want you inside me, Zachary,' she told him huskily.

'I'm beyond gentleness,' he warned through his teeth as if he wanted to make realise that he desired her too much.

'Good, because I'm beyond wanting it,' she said and leaped boldly up, trusting that he would catch her as she wound her legs around his narrow waist and leaned up to meet his heat-hazed and definitely not icy blue eyes with as much witchy invitation as she could get into one sizzling look to say, *Forget who I am supposed to be; make love to me until we are both sated and utterly, deliciously exhausted.*

Of course he caught her and of course he wanted her. She could feel just how much he wanted her as he carried her to the bed and followed her down so fast that even if she had been Caro she would have had no time to cool off with a little hitch of *Oh, no, what have I done?*

But she wasn't Caro. This was all Martha, the woman kissing Zachary back so hungrily that he forgot she was meant to be timid. He entered her wet and eager heat with such smooth, hard haste that Martha felt herself open all the way up to her heart. She was truly sunk now, wasn't she? She was drowning in feeling and pleasure and anticipation as he felt her hunger match his and consequently let his huge need join hands with her huge need, and they set a pace that blasted through all the doubts and fears he thought she should have.

He felt so good inside her that she let out a long moan of satisfaction, and the sound of it only made her feel more wrapped up in being Zachary's lover than she was before. She felt as wild for him as he obviously was for her, just as driven and every bit as desperate as he was, and so he deepened the already frantic rhythm of their sensually locked bodies and she went with him every step of the way. She was so hungry for this, so close to taking flight.

She heard herself moan and keen; maybe there were words and maybe it was only feral demands and more moans. She wasn't rational enough to hear her own thoughts let alone any words that came out of her mouth as he looked down into her eyes. His passionate, driven fascination with her written across his starkly handsome face was all the poetry she would ever need. The hard planes and sensitive angles of it looked just as she had imagined they might when in the throes of passion, and she couldn't help comparing the reality to her imaginings from that first time she had laid eyes on him and seen the sensual promise of his stern mouth despite his barely suppressed fury. Now it let her know how hard he was fighting his own need in order to push her over the edge into absolute delight before he took his own pleasure.

She thrashed her head back and forth on the coverlet as she felt that edge come so close she was almost touching it. Her body bowed with his to take him even deeper into her secret self as the pace changed and he thrust more strongly into her welcoming heat. She began to convulse around him even as shudders of pure ecstasy coursed through her and she let out a long, low-pitched moan of satisfaction as her core flexed in perfect time with his driving rhythm. She felt the deep, dark pulse of his wild release inside her as her own inner muscles tightened deliciously around his shaft and rippled with joy. They both went blank eyed as they were transported together into absolute ecstasy, and her moan of delight joined his groan of pleasure. The sound was the most perfect music to her.

As she drifted back down to earth, she felt him

rest his weight on his arms and her deliciously prone body for a long, lovely moment as the aftershocks of pleasure left her languorous and dazzled and utterly contented. She wanted this lovely intimacy with him to last forever, and she smiled against the salty skin of his neck as he strove to wrench breath back into his labouring lungs. She stretched lazily up to lick at the base of his throat as he bowed back in a last pulse of ecstasy. She deepened it to a kiss as she felt the pounding of his heartbeat under her mouth. It felt glorious to have been the one who had done this to him—she had made this mighty and supposedly aloof nobleman behave like a hot, fast and out-of-control lover with her.

Martha did this to you, Lord Elderwood, her wicked inner sensualist whispered in her heart of hearts. *Only Martha—Caroline had nothing to do with it.*

Even as he fought to recover from all that wonderful effort, she felt him begin to harden inside her all over again, as if he could never get enough of her. She smiled that wicked smile against his skin again in the hope it would encourage his enthusiasm for her, and he must have read her signal as a welcome for yet more delicious abandon. He leaned his head against hers for a moment longer but with what looked and felt like a mighty effort he then moved so he held his entire weight on his hands, as if he didn't want to relinquish their intimacy either. He stared down at her with such heat and with the memory of all that wild pleasure in his eyes. She wished she could have no secrets from her lover so she could return his guileless gaze of dazed wonder at what they had just done together with one of her own.

She could almost hear him reminding himself that they had a lifetime to do this again and again and that this would be enough for tonight. She badly wanted to argue with him—*no, there's only this moment*—but she couldn't. Before the world rushed back in and they had to renounce being lovers, it felt as if they still had a lovely cocoon wrapped around them, protecting them from the harsh reality outside his bedchamber door.

They had just made love, Martha reminded herself—as if she needed reminding. He had just made love to Mrs Martha Lington, not to Caroline, Lady Fetherall, and Martha let herself hope that a wild and instinctive part of him knew deep down that she wasn't her half-sister. His body knew she wasn't an abused woman too timid to love a powerful warrior like him freely, even if his brain had not yet caught up. He still thought he was going to marry Caro in the morning.

Martha, the deliriously delighted inner lover, tripped up midskip and fell on her happy little face as Lord Elderwood straightened his mighty arms and withdrew from his position of intimacy with the imposter in his bed. No, not in it, *on* it, she realised, and told herself she was shameless for only getting as far as the coverlet of his bed and not even down to the sheets. She felt the chill of January on her bare skin, even in this overheated house, and shivered with something far deeper than physical coldness. She wanted to stay locked in his arms until morning but it was impossible. She longed to make love with him all night long and only leave his bed when his valet came knocking on the door to get him ready for his wedding. *Then he would have to marry you anyway*, a sneaky inner voice argued with the rest of her.

By the time reluctant winter daylight pushed its way into Lord Elderwood's bedchamber tomorrow, she had to be long gone. She must run away from him and from this, as well as from Tolbourne. She needed to be well on her way back to Martha Lington's real life before the tardy winter dawn broke tomorrow. It felt as if the frost and greyness outside was making a hard lump of ice form inside her even as she watched Zachary rake out the dying fire and nurse it back to health. Even as that ice cooled her deliciously used body and dulled her eager senses, he was being the considerate soon-to-be husband of a woman who no longer even existed because surely Lady Fetherall must be Mrs Harmsley by now.

Martha eyed Caro's viscount as hungrily as a feral cat would a warm kitchen and a saucer of milk— desperate for the heat and taste but not daring to trust it wouldn't be snatched away the moment she reached for it. She was quite right; she wasn't for him and Viscount Elderwood wasn't for her. The end of her masquerade was galloping towards her at the speed of a runaway horse and she felt physical sadness, like a heavy weight on her shoulders, as she looked around her for something to wear so she could creep back to Caro's room and hope nobody was awake to spot Lady Fetherall dishevelled and dazed after half a night of passion with her nearly wedded husband.

Chapter Nine

Zach felt as if something more threatening than the cold of midwinter had crept into the room when his back was turned. Caroline had been a wild and deliciously uninhibited lover, and of course he hadn't been able to resist her passionate need and such urgent, unexpected sensuality. No, that was wrong; now he was passing his urgency off onto her. He couldn't protect himself from the firestorm of passionate need that had swept in. He had wanted her so much he would have struggled to hold himself back even if she had frozen in midkiss and decided she couldn't face a jot more intimacy.

He tried to tell himself he could have stopped if she had wanted him to, but a faint nausea in his belly argued it would have been a very close-run thing. He fought back a shiver of what felt like warning and decided this fire was alive enough to keep them warm for now. It was time to confront his demons and hers.

'What is it? What's the matter?' he asked when

he saw how her eyes were searching the shadows. They seemed even darker than usual as she watched him walking back to her with what looked like sadness and regret in her dark gaze. She could hardly pretend they were strangers after what they had just done but it might feel safer if they were. 'Did I hurt you?' he made himself ask her as horror gripped him at the thought of his raging passion for her delightful feminine body having harmed her in some clumsy way he wasn't aware of.

'No!' she gasped as if the very idea was impossible. 'You made me feel as if I could do anything if you were with me. As if we could climb to the stars together if we could find a ladder long enough.'

'Then what *is* the matter?'

'Nothing. Maybe I'm just exhausted,' she said as if she thought he might believe her fairy story. The woman he had just made love with had seemed capable of burning up with passion all night long and rising from his bed tomorrow morning fresh as a daisy, so why did he feel as if she wasn't going to?

'And maybe not,' he argued.

A few moments ago everything had been as natural as breathing between them as they lay naked together and temporarily sated. There didn't seem anything they couldn't do or say to one another, but now he felt as if too much of his true self was on show, and he could hardly stand here watching her like a satyr when she was still lying naked on his borrowed bed.

'I am a little bit,' she told him with a rueful smile

that seemed too half-hearted to be quite real. 'You are a very passionate man, Lord Elderwood,' she even managed to tease him almost lightly.

He had been almost desperate to make love to her when he had realised who had come knocking at his bedchamber door in the stilly watches of the night. Even now it only took a speculative look from her, a quick hint of wanting and wondering if he could do it again, for him to be very willing to try for a rematch. Maybe between them they could banish this feeling that everything they had just done together was slipping away like melting icicles through winter-numbed fingers.

Then one of the logs on the newly rebuilt fire sparked and flared behind the guard and it picked up an echo of itself at her feminine core. His heart skipped a heavy beat even as his body responded with intrigued eagerness to know even more about her innermost mysteries. It seemed unusual for such a dark-haired woman to have such a striking colour at her most intimate core, and Zach felt something significant shift in his memory.

He frowned as he tried to pin it down. He searched her beautiful face to see if she had noticed his gaze sharpen on her feminine centre and felt ashamed of himself for even thinking he had a right to speculate on whether it matched the rest of her. It felt intrusive of him but he couldn't help wondering about this passionate, secretive woman who was most definitely not what she seemed. Because of it, suspicion and an underlying dread pounded at his senses, demanding he use his brain instead of another part of his anatomy.

With a clearer head, he saw now that the kohl he had always thought Lady Fetherall used only to make her already fascinating dark eyes seem even more intriguing was smudged. Little wonder after their vigorous lovemaking and it seemed like a betrayal to think this way now, yet there was another hint of red under the blacking she had used on those impossibly long eyelashes of hers. He leaned closer, feeling like a traitor for acting like a jealous lover and thinking like an examining magistrate, but he had to know what was true and what was false about her now.

And suddenly it was all there, shocking in his memory, as an elusive and almost forgotten fact clicked into place and certainty followed. Underneath it all, she really was a redhead and not a brunette!

Fury lashed through him because he realised what that meant and because he felt so absolutely betrayed by the little witch. It meant she wasn't Lady Fetherall. Zach was as certain of it as if it had been written on her naked body while his back was turned. The old tale he had been told when this marriage had first been proposed to him said Lady Fetherall had been born with a redheaded sister of some kind, a little girl that Tolbourne legally disowned and sent to her mother's family in disgrace because he claimed she wasn't his son's child with a hair colour like that one. And yet the proof that Squire Tolbourne's son had most definitely fathered both of his daughters was lying sensually sated and still so deliciously feminine and fascinating on Zach's borrowed bed. The likeness between the half-sisters was truly astonishing. Even now that he knew who she really was, he found he had to blink several times before he could discern a difference between them. He could still be looking at her absent sister except for those hints of her true fiery hair colour in the flickering firelight.

He felt like such a damned fool for being so easily deceived. His eyes must have locked with *her* darkly mysterious gaze for the first time last week; at the time it had felt as if he had never truly seen her before, and now it was obvious he had not. Despite the shock he remembered experiencing at the time when he felt a glimmer of sensual interest in this woman who had never before excited the merest flicker of passion in him, he had ignored his instincts. She had walked down those stairs a week ago and he had had to fight a fierce blaze of desire.

What a fool she must think him! For how long had the real Lady Fetherall had this wicked deception planned? There had been no suggestion of inviting her sister to the wedding, even if the real Lady Fetherall had been brave enough to risk rousing her grandfather's fury by even mentioning the idea. Zach had been so reluctant and resentful about their marriage that he hadn't really cared to look twice at the woman to whom he would have to wed.

Which makes you a damned fool, he accused himself as his mystery woman's eyes evaded his gaze. Did she worry that he might read the secrets in her eyes? Didn't she know it was already too late for her to hide a single bit of herself from him? He had come to believe that he was starting out in marriage with a wife he could actually tolerate, could like and admire, and maybe even come to love. It had felt like such an unexpected blessing after he was all but forced into it by Tolbourne.

But nothing was as it seemed. Maybe to this sister—he couldn't even remember her name—he was only a quick bounce on a luxurious feather bed. She couldn't be planning to turn up in her sister's place and actually marry him, could she? No, that would turn a cruel masquerade into a crime and even now he couldn't think that badly of her.

All the same, the sting of the mockery he would endure when the world and his wife found out how royally he had been fooled by the counterfeit Lady Fetherall stoked his hurt to fury. This lying, cheating woman he had just made such fiery, passionate love with was nothing like the wronged woman Tolbourne had ruthlessly used as if she were a mere commodity in order to get his own way.

Zach tried his best to forget that this half-sister of Lady Fetherall had been rejected by the heartless villain as a child and branded a bastard. It was obvious the villain had lied since this woman was so like Lady Fetherall they could almost be twins. Tolbourne had blighted the life of his own granddaughter for some devious reason. If he wasn't careful, Zach would end up pitying the bewildered child she must have been instead of being furious with the woman she was now. He could go back to hating the old man later, but right now he had to deal with woman in front of him and not allow her to see how deeply she had hurt him.

'You have played me like a fish on a line, madam. I congratulate you. I never even realised how neatly I had been caught until this very moment,' he said coldly.

She flinched as if she had been stung and he wondered if she felt as exposed and undefended as he did.

'Here,' he said sharply, tossing his dressing gown at her. He tugged a discarded blanket off a nearby chair and used it to cover himself, although a suit of armour could hardly make him feel less vulnerable. 'You should have dyed that part of you as well as the rest if you expected to sneak into my bed in your sister's place without me realising I have just rutted with the wrong woman, madam,' he told her with a dismissive wave at her sex. His actions shamed him, but he was driven by a cold fury now.

His hurt fury wanted every bit of revenge it could get after she had made him believe that tonight was the beginning of far more for them than the four legs in a bed she must have intended it to be. Lord Elderwood didn't make love like that to women he wasn't due to marry in the morning, and that laid another layer of fury over the ones he already had sticking in his craw. She had made him into a lecher as well as a fool.

For a moment she seemed so shocked that he had found her out that she lay frozen on the bed on which they had just made such blissful love. He saw her shake suddenly, as if she had an ague, then control it with a fierce effort of will that threatened to make him ashamed of himself and beg her to forget he had been so harsh. Then she went from uneasy painted lady to offended queen in the blink of an eye and jumped off his bed as if she'd been scalded. She pulled the coverlet off to hide her nakedness and Zach felt it like a knife to his innards innards that she had refused to take something as personal as his dressing gown to cover herself up with. Now he had to be even more furious to guard himself from the pain of it.

'No, but that's a very good tip, my lord. I will be sure to remember it for next time,' she said, wrapped in her makeshift toga and defiant as a spitting cat.

Her goading twisted the knife and made him feel like a savage animal howling into the night. The idea of her tricking another deluded idiot her sister wanted to be rid of fuelled his anger. 'You two must have had a fine laugh at my expense all week, especially when I became so stupidly protective of Lady Fetherall, and she isn't even here for me to protect! I thought you were the one who had been at the mercy of a cruel grandparent for most of your life before he made you wed a brute. I even kept Tolbourne's lusty cronies at bay for you and you were never in any danger.'

'Yes, I was,' she said with a revolted grimace. 'They are brutes and I have been very glad of your protection from them, Lord Elderwood.'

'At least I was useful for something other than a good ride.'

She looked away as if his coarse words had devalued the breathtaking passion they had just shared and made him the worse for it. Of course they had, but everything he had believed he was sharing with her had been a lie. She had taken something important away from him and he didn't even want to think about what it was with her wary gaze on him. He wanted to turn his back on her and keep walking until he was far enough away to find a place where he could forget her and her devious half-sister, this stuffy, stifling house and its grasping owner. Unfortunately, it was the middle of the night and he was stark naked under his makeshift protection, so he stayed where he was, staring moodily at her.

He wasn't quite furious enough to strong-arm her out of his room and slam the door behind her, but maybe he could dress and leave this wretched place before the household was awake. He could leave Tolbourne and the wedding guests to find out that both the bridegroom and his lying bride had flown in the morning.

'Think what you like, Viscount Elderwood,' she said with a shrug, as if they were exchanging insults over a vast distance.

He shivered because suddenly that was how it felt. She looked magnificent as she glared defiance at him with her dyed-dark curls in a wilder tangle than ever bouncing on her bare shoulders and just a coverlet to hide her nakedness. Did he really want to be on the other side of a chasm from this woman who had lit the night with stars for him an impossibly short time ago? Yes, he decided, as stubborn desire for her threatened to unman him all over again. He wished he need never set eyes on her again if only for the sake of his sanity.

She had taught him to want things he'd thought he couldn't have. She had made him long for a marriage to which he had hated having to submit at the outset. Now, Tolbourne's ruthless plan to get himself a noble great-grandson he could boast about seemed like a minor sin compared to hers. She had made his world feel larger and more promising but it turned out his bride-to-be was a lie, and any reason she claimed could justify why she had done didn't seem very important next to that lie.

'Don't worry, I already am,' he replied shortly to that reckless invitation. 'I hope you and your sister enjoyed making a fool of me. You must have had a fine laugh at my stupid quest to open the heart of the real Lady Fetherall. As it turns out, you don't have a heart to find.'

'My sister does and she deserves better,' she said with a defiant shrug that said she loved her half-sister deeply.

This had better not be jealousy twisting in his gut because he wished she loved him instead. It could be fury—that was quite acceptable. He didn't want to be jealous of the strong sisterly bond that must have made this woman stand in her sister's place and pretend she was going to marry a noble idiot.

Deep down he knew he was wounded, that he felt more alone than ever before. He glared at her as all the stupid hopes she had opened inside him shattered like fine glass. No wonder it hurt. Her deception had made him so reckless that he had spent himself inside her... In an ironic twist of fate, he would have to marry her anyway now, just when he didn't want to.

Martha couldn't look at Zachary. He was so furious with her and clearly felt so wounded and wronged by her lies, yet he was still so wickedly desirable. She wanted to weep for the lovers they had just been. It had felt so truly intimate that this sudden turnaround was physically painful. She had always known he would end up hating her for what she had done to him, though, hadn't she?

She turned her head to stare into the shadows behind him. She refused to cry at his hard words and icy looks. Even if she did deserve it for lying to him, she wasn't made of stone and it hurt to hear him accuse her of laughing at him with Caro behind his back. She had never done that, and never would. He was to some degree right though; she had enjoyed this part of deceiving him. Not this part, not seeing his anguish and his pain after that breathtaking lovemaking. Not pretending that she was Caro and letting him think they could build a true marriage on such shaky foundations.

At least if Caro had managed to marry Harmsley, by now her sister would be able to enjoy the freedom that Martha's lies had paid for. Hopefully Caro would now be able to live her own life as she wanted to, but what about Martha? Yes, he was right. She couldn't lie to herself—she had enjoyed *this* part of her charade. *Enjoy* was too feeble a word for the fiery pleasure she and poor, deceived Zachary, Lord Elderwood, had just shared. Her body was still loose-limbed and languorous from that pleasure. She had gloried in him, soaked herself in the bliss of being his lover—lost herself in the fire and wonder of being made love to as if she were unique and infinitely precious to this mighty man. And what a superb lover he was to make even the cold dislike in his eyes now seem almost worth it for the glory of their precious moments together.

So yes, all of those things, and on top of that, the soaring, absolute joy of that incredible climax. She had enjoyed *this* part of the deception. After all, she would never have met him if she wasn't pretending to be Caro. That was the sad truth: she couldn't truly regret lying to him, in her heart of hearts, even now.

'I took no pleasure in deceiving *you*,' she said. That fine distinction was at least true, but he chose not to hear it.

'Yet you are so good at it. Almost a natural,' Lord Elderwood told her coldly and with a wave at her dyed hair, which was more dishevelled than ever, to make it clear there was very little else about her that *was* natural.

He was Lord Elderwood now, not Zachary. Maybe defying his cold-eyed haughtiness could help her get out of here with a few rags of her dignity left.

The thought of the powder and paint blurring until the real Martha fought past the false image of Caroline made her feel belittled and weak and unable to fight back, though, because she knew he was right. Yet Caro had spent nineteen years not being the person nature had intended her to be, so Martha refused to be ashamed of the reason why she was here. She shivered under her flimsy covering and felt so cold it was as if she would never be properly warm again.

'You don't know anything about me,' she still defended herself limply.

He looked as if the last thing he wanted was to know anything more. 'I soon will,' he said bleakly. She must have looked startled, because he went on as if she was a fool not to know what he meant. 'We will have to marry now,' he added, and she wondered if her ears were deceiving her.

'Of course we won't,' she protested. The very idea of marrying him when he had such hard dislike for her in his eyes again was impossible, and why should she?

'We do, and as soon as I can acquire a new special license,' he told her as if it was obvious. But why was she staring at him as if he was speaking an unknown language?

'Why on earth would I agree to marry a man who despises me?'

'Because of what has just passed between us, here in this room, on this bed. I had no...*self-control* while we were doing it. We must be wed now, whether we want to or not. That's the price we must pay for grabbing what we wanted like children in a sweetshop.'

'Well, I'm not paying it.'

'I would have thought you, of all people, should have more care for the hard lot of a child born out of wedlock.'

'But I *wasn't* born that way. It was only a wicked slander on my mother that Tolbourne made up because I refused to do as I was bid while Caro was so shy that she used to hide behind me. He wanted to get rid of me so he could take total control of my little sister's life before she was old enough to learn how to fight back, as I had. He thought up that lie to fool everyone that he was the wronged party instead of me. We were his only son's orphaned children and he used us like pawns on a chessboard.'

'How old were you when he sent you away?' Zachary asked almost gently, as if despite his fury he could see the pain and suffering that lie caused her.

'Six,' she said, feeling that bleak time sap her courage, when it was courage she desperately needed to face her current situation. 'Luckily my mother's family refused to believe his wicked slander against their beloved daughter, or I would have grown up in the Foundling Hospital and been taught to be ashamed of myself every day of my life until I left it for some other sort of drudgery, all because Tolbourne was already planning to push his only biddable grandchild into marrying a title one day.'

'Mine,' he pointed out grimly.

'Yours,' she agreed and suddenly she felt so tired.

All she wanted was to get away from him before she fell asleep on the bed on which they had done such wondrous things so recently.

Yet she had not sprung her sister from this trap only to be caught in it herself.

'How ironic that Tolbourne's rejected grand-daughter is the one who will end up as my viscount-ess. I might call it poetic justice if we weren't about to enter a marriage of pure necessity for the sake of the great-grandchild he always wanted.'

'No, we will not, because there's not the least need for us to marry,' she argued. The sorrow she had car-ried in her heart for the lack of Tom's child in her life felt more raw than ever because now she would also have to regret not having Zachary's either.

'No child of mine is going to be stigmatised as a bastard while I have breath left in my body to say the marriage vows to its mother, even if she has to be you.'

'There won't *be* a child. We have only shared a bed once and I can assure you it takes a lot more than that to make a baby.'

'No, it takes a lot less than what we just did to-gether, Madam Whoever-you-are.'

'No, it doesn't. Not with me,' she told him firmly, and somehow she had to make him believe her. She refused to marry him purely because His Lordship's honour demanded another sacrifice. 'I was married to my late husband for three years and didn't miss my monthly courses once in all that time. And, be-fore you start preening yourself on some inflated idea of your greater potency, I can assure you that we gave them plenty of cause to stay away when he was on leave from the navy.'

It sounded hard and a little vulgar but she had to make it plain to him that there was no reason why he should marry her against his will. She and Tom had loved one another but it was still a source of misery to Martha that she had not been able to give him even the hope of a pregnancy in her letters when he was away at sea. They had to wait weary months before they could be together again and hope for better luck next time. Then there were no more months, no more joyous leaves, no more next times. Not even the fading hope of a child after he was gone—just plain, blank nothingness. She shuddered at the memory of the absolute coldness of knowing there would never be a child to make her future seem more hopeful without Tom in it.

'How did he die?' Zachary said and once again his question was almost gentle. There was the good man under the protective fury again, and she wished so much that things had been different. And that wish felt dangerous.

She reminded herself of the agony of getting the letter that told her she was now a widow. It was still sharp; she didn't want to share it but she owed him an explanation. Tom had truly loved her, but Zachary was the man staring at her with guarded ice blue eyes and looking so remote that she wanted to cry.

'At Trafalgar,' she said with a lump in her throat

for the brutal ending of Tom's vigorous life and all their bright hopes for the future.

'He died a hero, then.'

'But he still died,' she said bitterly. 'I shall always be proud of him. He was a brave man who sacrificed his life for the freedom of his country, but I still have to live the rest of my life without him and without a child.' Tom had loved her so much that he had insisted it didn't matter if they never had children, and she was almost sure he had meant it. 'I have no intention of tying a viscount in need of an heir to a barren wife because we have been together just once.'

'Sometimes it only takes once, and my brother can deal with the succession if we don't happen to,' he said impatiently. He frowned down at her as if he actually wanted to wed her. What a stubborn and contrary viscount that would make him! It was a good thing she didn't believe him.

'He won't have to because I'm *not* going to marry you,' she insisted. 'I refuse to let you make a noble sacrifice because you think your precious honour demands it. That's how we got into this mess in the first place. It's why you were going to marry my sister without even trying to love her as she deserves to be loved.'

'Noble sacrifice be damned! You have to marry me because there's still a chance I have got you with child, despite your previous marriage and all that trying you did with your late husband,' he insisted, but then he would, wouldn't he?

He was a proud and honourable man who made her

feel like a dishonourable woman—just not quite dishonourable enough to marry him. 'No, I shall never be wed again and certainly not to you, Lord Elderwood.'

'Why not?'

'Let's start with the scandal that my own grandfather threw at me nineteen years ago. Tom ignored it and married me anyway but he wasn't a viscount. Then we can add the fact that I have too much to do at home to leave the grandparents who did own me when Tolbourne would not, despite the scandal, in the lurch. Next, there's the fact that you would be ashamed to name me as your wife. If you need more reasons, we could always add that I am a liar and a deceiver. That sounds like plenty of reasons why it's impossible for Viscount Elderwood to marry plain old Mrs Martha Lington.'

'A baby feels like a good enough reason to me,' he said stubbornly. Ultimately, that was this was about, wasn't it?

'Well, it's not. It's stubborn foolishness for you to even imagine there will be one after what I have just told you. You hate me for lying to you and I will not be trapped in a marriage with you just because you think yourself more of a man than my Tom was when that simply is not true.'

'Do you still love him?'

'Of course I do. Love doesn't stop because someone dies; that's why it hurts so much,' she said, and it was true. She was also terribly afraid that she could love this man if only he would let her, and that would make it such an unequal marriage that she couldn't even contemplate it.

'I am sorry for your loss,' he said stiffly.

'Thank you.'

'My mother would agree with you about the hurt. She still mourns my father to this day, although he died fifteen years ago. I always wanted to love my wife as deeply as he loved her,' said the man who came here to marry Caro, but certainly not for love.

'Then we are definitely not getting married, and I shudder to think what your mother would say if we did. I trail a scandal after my name no loving mother would want for her grandchildren, even if we had any, which we wouldn't.'

'You could certainly match my mother for stubbornness, even if you don't love me as she did my father. He was impoverished and her family didn't approve of the match one bit but gave in when she insisted it was him or nobody for her.'

'And you want to wed me for so much less than they had? It's as well I won't let you,' she said as the contrast between his parents' marriage and the one he was telling her they must have could not have felt stronger, or less loving.

'*Let* me?' he said, offended by the idea she was in charge but she had to be.

'I will *not* marry you, my lord.'

'You might as well, since the love of your life is no longer with us. You have nothing to lose,' he said almost sulkily.

She had to fight a smile that might encourage him

to think she would weaken and agree to marry him, just because he had got the idea fixed in his head and was too stubborn to admit she was right.

'Only everything,' she murmured and hoped he hadn't heard.

She had come up against his stubborn pride, and nothing she said seemed to move him now that he had decided marrying her was the honourable thing to do. Let him be stubborn, then; she was too tired to argue with him again and she needed to be on her way if she was to be gone before morning. Even Lord Elderwood couldn't marry a woman who wasn't here for him to marry.

'Think what you like,' she said wearily. 'I need my bed.'

'You can sleep here,' he said with a careless wave at the bed in which they had been such enthusiastic lovers a heartbreakingly short a time ago.

How did he think she could sleep with him after all they had done and said to one another tonight? Did he really expect her to topple onto it and find oblivion lying next to him after she had experienced such…such, well, ecstasy, transformation, bliss with him?

No, don't try to work out exactly what it was, Martha—just get out of here while you still can. You can't lie next to him for the rest of your lives. You can't give him an heir and you don't even want to marry the man, do you?

'No,' she said, backing away from the bed and shaking her head all the way to the doorway, until she bumped into the door handle behind her. She jumped as if her wicked grandfather had prodded her in the back with a sharp stick; as if even his house wanted him to have a titled great-grandchild, and that was never going to happen now. 'I can't stay here. I can't sleep with you,' she said and heard the note of hysteria in her own voice and bit her lip to stop betraying her agitation.

He must have heard it too as his gaze went wary, as if he thought she was about to have hysterics. Well, let him think it; she wanted to get away so desperately that her feet were moving even as her eyes lingered on his austerely handsome face as she tried to memorise it in minute detail. She wanted to fix his image in her head because she would never see him again.

'I need to think,' she lied, but really she had to get away before he trapped them in a worse marriage than even he had expected when he came here.

'Very well. Go and get some sleep. We both need to be ready for a busy day tomorrow. We will have to set off to London as soon as it is light so we can get our special license at Lambeth Palace on the way to Flaxonby.'

Too heartsick and weary to argue with him any more, Martha took one last look at Zachary Chilton being lordly and commanding and ridiculously desirable—and still she refused to cry. If she'd had any intention of marrying him, why did he think she would do it from his home and not hers? *Arrogant, cocksure, irritating man*, she silently called him. How sorely they would have tried each other's patience if she had been fool enough to stay here and marry him.

'Don't bother packing any more of your sister's clothes than you need to stand up in. We can order more when we get to Bond Street,' he told her, as if he still thought he was going to marry her in a few days.

'Goodnight, my Lord,' she said firmly and left the room with his murmured reply echoing in her ears. *Sweet dreams, my lady...*

He was such an arrogant devil she almost wished she had never met him.

Chapter Ten

He was a damned fool, Zach decided the next morning when he found out that his unexpected bride had flown in the night. He had sat around for most of the morning like an idiot, and she had left so stealthily he hadn't heard a thing. She would have had her escape plan worked out when she came here, and it would be nigh on impossible to follow the devious woman's trail by now.

So that was that, then. She didn't want to marry him and he didn't want to marry her—stalemate. Of course he didn't want to wed a woman who was still in love with her late husband, the dead hero of the greatest sea battle in decades, if not centuries. Martha must have married this Lington fellow out of the schoolroom if the fellow died five years ago. By his reckoning, Mrs Martha Lington must be five and twenty now if she was six when Tolbourne threw her out of this house nineteen years ago. Apparently

she had left Zach with a few of his wits since he re-
tained those bare facts after their argument last night.

Not very many, he decided, as his failure to convince her to marry him ground into his pride and
into something far deeper he didn't want to think
about. He did think of his mother, still so in love
with his father all these years after his death, and, if
he wasn't so angry with his runaway lover, he might
despair. An alive, stay-at-home-and-do-his-duty viscount wasn't much competition for her sainted hero
husband, was he? He wasn't going to think about
her again, though, was he? He was going to accept
her desertion as final and get on with his life without her. He was going to be deliriously happy not to
have ended up married to either Tolbourne sister.

Yet here he was still thinking of her even though
he knew he was well rid of her. He paced the room
while his valet tried to pack with him cluttering up
the room being furious with a woman who wasn't
even here for him to be furious with. If he wasn't
careful he wouldn't have a manservant or a groom
left to put up with his grim moods and foul temper.

So neither Tolbourne sister wanted to marry him?
So what? There were plenty more fish in the sea. Except this hollow feeling inside said he didn't want any
of them; he only wanted the one he had made love to
last night. He struggled with the lowering feeling that
she might have been remembering her darling Tom
while they made hot, sweet love together. He could
have sworn she had been thinking only of him, that

she had been with him every step of the way as his glorious, passionate, unforgettable lover.

Not unforgettable. Please let her not be that. Please let her be just the most stubborn, contrary, elusive female I have ever encountered and probably will never see again.

It finally occurred to him to remember to ask himself why Lady Fetherall had needed a week during which nobody knew she was missing but her sister and her lady's maid. Possibly those rumours of a secret lover were true, but Martha was the sister with all the fire and spirit. He still longed for her despite her lies and despite his inner cynic insisting that both sisters were likely engaged with lovers, that both sisters must be devious to think of playing such a trick on him. *His* Tolbourne sister—when had he started to think of Martha as *his*?—was stubborn as a mule and very protective of her younger sister. Zach, the deserted lover, wanted to rage and curse and throw things, but even he could not convince himself that there was nothing more to Martha's deception than a cruel trick played by two loose sisters.

He had to get out of here with at least a shadow of his pride intact. He would be the actor this time, the viscount pretending to be mildly amused and even secretly relieved that Lady Fetherall had bolted in the night rather than marry him.

'I'll track the little tramp down, Elderwood,' Tolbourne barked despite their eager audience. 'Just an attack of wedding day nerves,' he added after a nervous titter from one of the ladies who were witnessing this delicious spectacle. 'You know what fools women can be at times like this,' Tolbourne blustered, as if he had never given himself away in public by calling his granddaughter a foul name.

There was such flinty fury in his eyes as he played with his riding whip, as if his granddaughter would suffer a lot more than an attack of the vapours when he caught up with her. Zach might want to be furious with Lady Fetherall and her sister, but he didn't want them to be caught by a man without scruples or an iota of love in his heart for anyone else but himself.

'Just let the lady go where she pleases, Tolbourne,' he said icily. 'I wouldn't marry Lady Fetherall now if you threatened to blast Holdfast Castle off the face of the earth and half of Northumberland with it. I will never say yes to her again; you have my solemn promise on it and I am a man of my word.'

'But you want the place back in your family so badly you agreed to wed a—'

Zach decided to stop the man before he betrayed more contempt for his granddaughter in public. 'I already wished myself out of the agreement before this, and I am grateful to Lady Fetherall for saving us both from a lifetime of unhappiness. Good day to you all, ladies and gentlemen,' he added with a mocking bow at the fascinated onlookers, then he strode across the stable yard to take Thor's reins. At least the sight of a stallion dancing and prancing should make them give him a wide berth.

Zach frowned at the thought of Tolbourne's

threats. He knew they were not hollow ones made out of a fury that would soon fade. He meant them, so it was impossible for Zach to ride hell for leather all the way back to Flaxonby and forget both Tolbourne sisters as fast as possible after all. Somehow he had to find a way to protect both sisters from their unnatural grandparent's wrath, even if it would have to be from afar.

He rode away from Tolbourne House with a sigh of relief; Lady Fetherall—or Mrs Lington, as he must now think of her—was no longer in his presence or in his life and he would neither lust after nor worry about her. He could almost admire her effrontery and that clever impersonation if he didn't feel as if something unique and precious had been trampled underfoot last night. If he let himself think too hard about their prickly confrontation it would hurt like hell, but he watched the January countryside flash by under Thor's eager hooves and brooded about the child Mrs Martha was so certain they could not have, even if she wanted them to. But he wanted it. He wanted her to be the mother of his children, her and only her, and that conclusion really worried him.

Even if he could catch up with her on the devious trail she would have been so careful not to leave for him or Tolbourne to follow, they were already at check. He had offered to marry her and she had said no. He had said he wanted her children but she had said she couldn't have any. She would still say no to him, even if he did find her and beg instead of order her to be his viscountess, never mind the silly differences she wanted to make between his rank and hers.

She didn't have enough faith in them together to take the risk, to believe it really wouldn't matter to him if his brother's children had to carry his title on one day. But if he did find her and beg for that much, he would have to be certain of his own feelings, and he wasn't certain of anything right now. He would need to be in love with her and he wasn't prepared to be that foolish, not even for her or the baby she was so sure she wouldn't have.

He had a week's worth of deception and lies to get past and even then the idea of loving such a woman was enough to send him back to London screaming. And all that aside, how could he have any hope of bludgeoning his way into her affections with the ghost of her husband standing between them?

It took Martha nearly a fortnight to get home. She made her way back there by several indirect routes in order to avoid Tolbourne's furious pursuit and maybe Lord Elderwood's as well. She had planned her journeys to go first in one direction then another and changed her name and appearance several times. At last she was almost herself again and nearly home so her zigzag path must have kept Tolbourne's thugs and Zachary off her tail. Maybe they had already lost interest in her, although they would only have to lie in wait for her near Greygil if they hadn't, but she couldn't stay away from her home any longer. She had been gone too long as it was and was desperate to see her grandparents again.

Furthermore, she needed to find out whether Caro and Mr Harmsley were married. Martha had done all she could to help them and now she believed good news would be waiting for her at Greygil— and hoped to hear that their plan had worked. Caro would be out of Tolbourne's reach at long last and that was all this misadventure had been about. Soon it would feel like an unreal interlude in her normal busy life, and her week of being someone very different would fade to an unlikely memory. It was possible, but it seemed unlikely. It felt more like her time in Kent pretending to be betrothed to the reluctant Viscount Elderwood was vivid reality and this, her real life, was fiction.

She stared moodily out of the window of the coach and wondered why all the life and bustle of towns and cities along her way had seemed so dull because they couldn't outdo the images in her head. Calling him by his title ought to make Zachary stiff and aloof, less of a real man and just a lord like all the others. It ought to, but it didn't. Even that first night, when he was so furious about the trap he thought he'd been caught in, he had been so full of life and frustrated energy he had been unforgettable. She smiled at nothing as she recalled the banked-down temper in his extraordinary eyes and felt an echo of the shiver she felt the first time she met him.

She was a fool to think he was ever going to fade

into a dim memory. He was so confoundedly handsome; there should be a rule somewhere that said nobody as powerfully built and tempting could become a viscount. She sighed and felt the shadow of all the years of secretly missing the wretched man yawning ahead of her. By now, he had probably shrugged his shoulders and decided to forget her and the whole humiliating business of his failed engagement to Lady Fetherall, but something told her she was never going to be able to forget him.

But for now, she had to get ready to pretend nothing was amiss when she got home. If she didn't learn to hide it better, her grandmother's sharp eyes would soon pick up on her preoccupation with a man Martha Lington should never have let herself want in the first place. Nobody knew or cared what a stranger was thinking or longing for as she wound her slow way towards home, but Grandmama would, and Grandfather Winton could even pick up on the wobble in her smile or a passing sadness in her eyes and start to worry about her. She could not let that happen. Grandfather was a decade older than Grandmama and not very inclined to slow down and admit he wasn't as fit as he used to be. Time to put Zachary into a corner of her mind and do her best to wall him off from the life she was going back to, the home she loved and the grandparents who had loved her when nobody else had wanted to.

Reminded of her other grandfather, the one she didn't want to admit to, Martha wondered uneasily what Tolbourne was doing. Surely, given the delightful scandal the *ton* must be laughing about by now, he would admit defeat and let her sister go? She shivered and hoped so. Once Caro was a wealthy country gentleman's wife, and mother to his child, what could Tolbourne do but accept her marriage or look a fool for being furious that her new husband didn't have a title? Another shiver said he could still lash out in his frustrated fury at either of them, but she refused to consider that idea seriously or she might have to spend her life in fear of him.

How Lord Elderwood's ears must be burning at being the object of so much gossip. How he must despise her for what she had done to his pride. She squirmed in her seat at the thought of him having to pretend he didn't care what they said about him. Having seen the real Zachary under the lordly armour, she knew he would care, knew he would hate it if that gossip damaged his family after all they had been through to try to rebuild their reputation.

She too was sensitive about those she loved and still felt angry that he had judged her sister by the false image Tolbourne had made Caro show the world. Maybe he had been protecting himself by not looking harder at Caro and seeing that she had been forced into that engagement even more ruthlessly than he had been. What he had thought as he put the Chilton emerald on Caro's ring finger hardly mattered now. He was back in his world and Martha was about to return to hers.

She sighed at the hollow that distance from him had opened up in her heart. She told herself he was in the past now, just a dream that another Martha in another life might have been able to hold on to, but in this Martha had to let him go.

He had not come chasing after her so he must agree. He was so stubborn that if he wanted to she had no doubt he could have found her, however clever her avoidance tactics were. How he must be congratulating himself on a lucky escape. She had refused his gallant offer of marriage, but the magnificent scenery outside the carriage windows still blurred as she recalled Zachary's starkly handsome face transformed by pure desire. She wanted to cry for the loneliness of never seeing him like that again. The sad truth was that she longed for him to whisper of love and trail seductive kisses down her body. She blinked away a furtive tear and made herself concentrate on the march of familiar landmarks that signalled her home was getting closer.

Then the coach stopped at the nearest halt to Greygil to let her off. She felt too restless and impatient to wait for the inn trap to come back from its errand or send for Grandfather's gig so she walked from the village. As she trudged up the drive to Greygil Manor House at long last, her home had never looked dearer. There were no snowdrops or shy primroses in bloom here to say that spring would soon be on its way, but life felt so much more right and true here than it had at Tolbourne House. This was where she belonged.

The Martha who was coming home now felt like a different woman from the one who had set off nearly six weeks ago. It had been just after Christmas when she had set out in response to an urgent summons from her sister. She'd had no idea what had lain ahead of her back then, but she had always been happy to spend a few snatched hours or days with her half-sister, however it could be arranged. Her grandparents would hate all the lying she had done while she was away, even if it was for a good cause. They would forgive her in time, especially if Caro was happy. They had always been concerned for Papa's other daughter because they were good people and knew Tolbourne was ruthless to the bone.

Martha decided she would tell them everything— except that she had lain with Zachary—about the strangest of weeks at Tolbourne House. She knew she couldn't share all of the glories and hurts of it even with them; some secrets did more damage in the telling than in the keeping. She felt her cheeks flush at that last lie by omission, but at least she had the excuse of her walk up the drive from the village to hide behind. Maybe she would begin to feel right about herself and her true place in life soon—so long as she made herself forget she had met a viscount who could make her heart race with only a questioning look or wry smile. Zachary truly had set the stars spinning for her before he had found out the truth and brought them both crashing back to earth with a bruising thud. He was Lord Elderwood and she was a simple country widow.

'Martha! Oh, thank heavens you're home at long last,' her grandmother exclaimed, and Martha realised she had been so deep in thought that she had walked around the house to the back door without even thinking about it.

'It's wonderful to be home, Grandmama,' she said as they hugged, and Martha felt truly as if she was home. This was the place she belonged, with the people she loved and who loved her. Her darling grandmother was wearing an apron with traces of baking day on it and there was flour in her grey hair, but she was security and familiarity and home. Martha burst into tears. 'I'm so sorry. I can't think what's come over me.'

'Weariness and seeing that wicked man again, I should think,' her grandmother said bracingly and handed Martha a spotless lawn and lace handkerchief from her apron pocket. That was Grandmama all over—comfort and safety overlaid with common sense and just a hint of ladylike frivolity.

'You know where I've been, then? Caro got a message to you? Is she married?'

'Aye and she sounded happy as a dog with two tails in the letter. Her husband rode over with it since your sister won't be in a fit state to travel for a few months.'

'Ah, he told you about the baby as well, then.'

'Your sister insisted we had to know everything before the gossip about what you had been up to when you were down south reached us. She's a good girl, despite the mess she got you tangled up in. At least now she's going to be living near Harrogate and you won't have to trail off to London to see her anymore.'

'That's a blessing,' Martha agreed, and it probably was. 'About my hair,' she said to distract herself from the idea she might have glimpsed Zachary from a distance if she had still had to go to London to meet Caro. A chance sighting of him in the park or on a stroll down Bond Street wouldn't help her to forget him so it was just as well she need never go there again.

'Your grandfather will be horrified, Martha. Couldn't you have worn a wig?'

'Imagine it sliding askew or even flying off while I was riding.'

'We used to wear them when I was a girl and mine never did, although I did used to feel as if I had a round loaf or two piled up on my head sometimes.'

'I couldn't have coped with that as well as pretending to be Caro. I'm afraid the colour won't wash out. Will you help me to cut it off before Grandpapa sees it, Grandmama?'

'You'll look like a skinned rabbit.'

'I need to be done with all that lying,' Martha said bleakly. Her grandmother gave her a long look, and Martha knew there were shadows under her eyes that had not escaped her grandmother's keen notice. 'Better to be a bald Martha than a fake Caroline,' she tried to joke.

'I'd settle for you being happy, my love.'

'I am. My sister can be her own woman at last, so of course I'm happy.'

'As if I don't know my own grandchild! But maybe in time you'll tell me what really happened to you in that awful man's house.'

'Maybe,' Martha said, but she doubted it. 'Where is Grandfather?'

'Where do you think?'

'Out on the fells. Now I know I have been gone too long,' Martha said and felt her old life slipping back into place all around her. Her grandmother ushered her into the scullery and snipped away at her hair. More and more of it fell in a stiff heap of dark curls around Martha's feet and she tried not to remember how it was before it'd had to be dyed with stronger and stronger dyes to hide its bright colour.

'We'll tell him you picked up lice travelling on the stage and we had to cut it off,' her grandmother said when as much of it had gone as she could bring herself to cut off. 'You can wear a scarf to hide what's left until it grows back.'

'Luckily he thinks anywhere south of Kendal is full of unwashed barbarians so I expect he'll believe it.'

'He might be right about the barbarian part, given the state you've come back to us in.'

'I'm perfectly all right, Grandmama. There's nothing wrong with me that a few nights of restful sleep won't put right.'

'I doubt it, but we'll see.'

Chapter Eleven

Determined to put Zachary Chilton out of her mind, along with the unreal week she had spent pretending to be Caro, Martha threw herself back into walking or riding the fells on her grandfather's business. Yet, being set on doing something and actually doing it turned out to be very different things. Zachary was proving to be stubbornly unforgettable so far.

The changes in the weather should have kept her so busy she had no time left over for brooding about dangerously handsome noblemen who should stay in the past where they belonged. Yet it might as well have been glorious midsummer for all the difference this foul weather made to her vivid memories of him. She had discovered that it was perfectly possible to think too much and work hard at the same time amidst rain of such unrelenting fury that it was a struggle to keep even the tough hill sheep properly fed and healthy in the midst of mud and bitter winds and the everyday cold of February. Bringing the sheep to lower ground so they could feed and tend to the pregnant ewes took so much time and energy that Martha was glad to fall into bed at night and sleep from sheer exhaustion; at least on those days she was too tired to dream.

The wild storms made their lives hard enough but they were followed by heavy snow. Battling the relentless cold and bitter winds between each blizzard made everything take twice as long. How stupid of her to long for Zachary's strong arms around her and his strength at her back while she fought her way through the drifts. But she must keep going to make sure Grandfather Winton didn't join in her daily battle with the elements.

At the peak of the bad weather she even had to spend most of a day and a night in a barn with her grandfather's most prized flock of sheep when she and the dogs were caught out in the fiercest blizzard she had ever experienced. Marooned halfway up a fell in its stoutly built shelter, she stuffed straw into as many cracks in the doors and shutters as she could to keep the snow out. She had plenty of time to worry about how her grandparents would be worrying about her as she sat in her nest of straw with the dogs huddled in for warmth, and there was nothing left to do but wonder why she felt so bereft. Tom was always an ache in her heart she would never entirely forget, but he had been her youthful love. It felt as if he was slipping away from her as she sat there feeling exhausted and a little bit hopeless, as every day of her five and twenty years of life lay heavy on her shoulders. She knew that was ridiculous—she was still young—she just didn't feel like it.

Then there was Zachary. She had lost him too, although at least he was still alive. That was something to be happy about, even if she never saw him again. Confound the man for being such a fine lover! The fire they had stirred up between them threatened to blot everything else from her mind. She had been right to turn him down; she would do it again if he walked through these snow-buffeted old doors right now. Even if he knelt at her feet and said he loved her and begged her to marry him, she would have to act the hard woman and turn him away because she was barren.

She eyed the swollen flanks of the ewes and pictured the new lambs due in a couple of months' time. Thank goodness there was nobody here but the dogs to see her weep for the babies she would never have. She told herself she was crying for the children she had not been able to give Tom, the comfort she could have got from raising them, even without him. For once let herself feel the terrible sadness the lack of them caused her, and some of her grief for her tragically young husband along with it. Miles away from home and with the blizzard still raging, she could cry without worrying that her grandparents would hear her.

It wasn't the dogs' fault she longed for one very particular pair of masculine arms to hold her close and comfort her instead of their furry bodies anxiously wriggling even closer. She wanted the deep rumble of Zachary's voice as he stroked her short hair and whispered comfort, but he was half a country away. He was probably at a party or the theatre, or even making love to another woman right now.

She cried even harder at that idea and still wished he would appear to hold her while she mourned for the children she would never have. Despite wallowing in misery, she managed a weak chuckle at the thought of him in his exquisitely tailored Bond Street finery and fastidiously clean linen fighting his way through a blizzard to join her in a barn full of sheep. Then she pictured him wet through and out of temper as he cursed her for living so far off the beaten track because look at the state he had got himself in while he was finding her.

'Foolish man,' she chided. She was shocked to hear how husky and tear-muffled her voice sounded, and longed for the comfort of his vital presence even more.

'Stupid woman,' she chided herself, but she still smiled at the thought of him as she drifted off to sleep.

Zach had refused to see Tolbourne since he returned to London. He had too much brooding to get through over the most stubborn, contrary and unforgettable woman he had ever met to bother about the old villain. Zach had Martha Lington's wrongs to be outraged about as well as his own now, and he was afraid he really would lay violent hands on the viper if he let him in. He was furious on her behalf for the baseless accusations against her mother that Martha had endured as a little child, just so Tolbourne could push her out of his life and not seem the villain he was for doing it.

Zach also had every agent he could trust raking through Tolbourne's life for secrets, or more lies, to use to keep him away from the new Mrs Harmsley and the stubborn Mrs Lington. It felt as if it was his duty to make sure the old man had no chance to take revenge on them for the trick they had played.

Now that he was rational again, he was grateful they had deceived him. He had never wanted to marry Caroline, but he had been eager to marry her half-sister. He had wished he had let his temper cool before he had let his hurt feelings out and made her think he was only offering to marry her because there could be a child. The sad truth was that he wanted Martha; he wanted her so instantly and completely that he should have known it was more than lust. He recalled how it had felt to meet her eyes for the first time with all the contradictions and challenges he had never seen in Lady Fetherall's wary gaze. That night his heart had seemed to stop for a frantic moment; breath had jammed in his lungs as the whole world went still and silent around them. Then he had seen her barely there silk gown, tousled hair and painted face, and had felt the old outrage that he was being forced to marry a cynical husband hunter in order to regain what should have been his birthright. Instinct might have been screaming she

was not what she seemed, but arrogant Viscount Elderwood had refused to listen.

He might want to kick himself for his stupidity
now, but going over it in his head day after weary day
was doing him no good at all. He had a family to look
out for, and a large estate to keep running as justly
as he could but still at a profit. He had the rest of his
life to get on with without the woman he…wanted;
that was it—*he wanted her*. That night Martha had
wanted him too but she had soon changed her mind.

She might not want to marry him, but he could
at least make sure she was safe in her beloved Cumberland. He had sent his lawyer to inform Tolbourne
that evidence against him was lodged in several safe
places with orders to unseal and publish if he ever
tried to harm his granddaughters in any way. He had
done what he could to keep her and her sister safe
and happy, so now he ought to be able to forget the
whole sorry business.

It wasn't as if he would have been able to match
her youthful, heroic and annoyingly popular Lieutenant Lington even if she had said yes to him. He
had made it his business to find out about that promising young naval officer who had been cut off in
his prime, but in this case knowledge wasn't power;
it just made him feel worse. Even hardbitten sailors
grew sentimental as they described to him how much
Lington and his beautiful young wife had adored one
another and did he know they had been childhood
sweethearts? Zach found out he was jealous of a dead

paragon whom Martha still loved, and it should have helped him to forget her, but it did not.

Instead, best think about Tolbourne's offer to sell him Holdfast Castle and estate after all, then. Zach had thought the man would rather give it to the boot boy than sell it to the man who had threatened to expose his shady dealings, but apparently profit outran personal feelings; Zach was beginning to doubt Tolbourne had any feelings. Now he had disowned both granddaughters, Zach wondered if the old man planned to take his money with him to the grave. The real question was whether Zach needed Holdfast so badly that he was willing to pay a ridiculously inflated price for it. The old man's new bitterness against both of his granddaughters had made him disown Caroline as well. Now he was willing to let Holdfast go at last and Zach was no longer sure that he wanted it.

At least Martha had taught him to think much harder about what really mattered in life. She had taken a huge risk to help her sister marry the man she loved. She had reminded him that people were more important than a pile of ancient stones. Now he must think his way past the duty he had always put first; if Tolbourne was not going to be allowed to rule his granddaughters' lives in future, maybe Zach's father and grandmother should not dictate his from the grave either. He was the head of the Chilton family; his title and estate meant that they were the real centre of his world.

It was time he consulted his mother, brother and

little sister about Tolbourne's offer to sell him Hold-fast and see whether they thought it was too high a price to pay. Maybe this time he could listen to them, and they could all truly put the past behind them at long last.

It was well into March before Martha decided she could not lie to herself for a moment longer. The courses that she had told Zachary were relentlessly prompt had now failed to arrive for the second time. The dragging tiredness she had tried to convince herself was caused by too much emotion during what now seemed an almost dreamlike week in Kent and so much hard work since she got back, was really being caused by something else. Fatigue occasionally threatened to overwhelm her so badly it was sometimes a great effort to get up the stairs of an evening before she fell onto her bed and slept as if her life depended on it. Her nipples were so wincingly sensitive she thought she might cry out and give too much away if she even moved the wrong way against her heavy winter clothing. Tears came far too easily if she didn't distract herself with work. It was high time she admitted she was wrong and Zachary could well have been right that night.

She could be carrying his child. No, never mind *could be*; she was. After just one single, very passionate encounter with Viscount Elderwood, she was increasing. Why on earth had she been so sure it had been safe to snatch that one wondrous lovemaking with Zachary before he found out who she really was? That was the heart of the problem, though, wasn't it? She was Martha and not Caroline. She was the long-rejected sister, cast off by her own father's father and legally disinherited. She was as unsuitable a wife for a viscount as it was possible for her to be without actually being born in the streets. The mud Tolbourne had thrown at his own grandchild still clung, despite Tom's honourable life and death and his rock steady determination to marry her anyway.

She nearly cried again but instead shook her head impatiently and loved her Winton grandparents more than ever for taking her in and loving her despite all that mud. Now she was about to shame them again and this time it was her own fault. Yet even as she looked the future in the face, she knew she couldn't pretend she hadn't enjoyed every last second of making this baby with a viscount whom her sister was supposed to have wed the next day.

Sickness threatened again as the harsh reality behind that lovely fantasy stole back in and bit her. She fought the nausea in case someone heard her up here in her room retching miserably and put two and two together. She made herself sit back on the bed and work out how long she had to go before the whole world knew she was with child and not married to the father. At least she knew exactly when her child had been conceived so all she needed to do now was find out a great deal more about how a human baby progressed in the womb. Then maybe she would feel more prepared to become this one's mother in seven months' time.

She felt the changes her baby was already making to her body but at least there was no visible sign of it on the outside yet. Although she couldn't quite believe Mother Nature had played such a trick on her after three long years of barren marriage to Tom, and even though she was carrying another man's child, part of her was overjoyed—the part that wasn't shocked and surprised and a little bit terrified of what just one night with a viscount had done to all three of them.

She was growing Zachary's child inside her and she was going to have to seek him out and tell him so. He was going to be a father in a few months' time whether he wanted to be one or not; perhaps she could swallow her pride and beg him to marry her for the baby's sake. She must leave home before her condition showed if she was not to bring shame on her grandparents, but in any case finding him came first. Even before telling Grandfather and Grandmama she must tell the child's father. She couldn't hide her sickness and soreness from the sharp eyes of her grandmother for much longer, so she had to do it soon.

If he wanted no more to do with her or was already looking for a very different wife, Martha still could not put her grandparents through the ordeal of watching their granddaughter openly carry a viscount's bastard. Not after they had taken her in against the advice of so many former friends when Tolbourne had cast her out as a bastard herself. If she stayed here she would have to raise the little mite with that stigma miring its life as well as hers, and she already loved it far too much to inflict such a fate on it.

Somehow it could be managed discreetly if Zachary turned the same hostile, angry ice blue stare on her as he had that first night at Tolbourne House and rejected them both after the humiliation of her deceit and trickery. She could invent a dying godmother or a burning desire to pay a long visit to some of her old naval friends if she had to. Grandmama would think of an obscure branch of her family she could kill off and leave them with a tiny little orphan who had nobody else to care for it if that was the way it had to be, but first Zachary must know he was going to be a father.

Martha put a protective hand against her heaving but still very flat stomach and swore to give her baby the best life she possibly could. To do that she would have to track down Zachary and beg him to marry her, even if he now spurned her for fleeing Tolbourne House without leaving him so much as a note. Their child was more important than her pride and all the reasons they should not wed one another. The idea of raising a child in a not very convenient marriage that its father was sure to resent might not feel ideal, but it was better than her child growing up illegitimate and scorned for its parents' sins—all because she had been so convinced she could not bear a child. Her night of exquisite passion with her sister's unwanted fiancé really had been exquisite, though, hadn't it? Even now she couldn't fool herself into believing it was anything but extraordinary for her but now they would both pay a high price for that night.

He was a man of honour so he would probably see them both as his duty and do what he saw as the decent thing. He would never feel such fiery, driven ardour for her again because of what she had done, but he was a true gentleman. His family's honour and his duty had got them into this mess in the first place so it would probably get him trapped again—and by her this time. All because he refused to turn his back on a promise to his dead grandmother.

Zachary had ended up engaged to Caro. He thought it didn't matter if they allowed their passion for one another to reach the most exquisite climax she had ever experienced in her life because as far as he knew she would be his wife the next day; she had believed the same, but for a very different reason. Now her reckless arrogance could cost him his freedom, and the thought of it made her feel so sick she had to dash to her wash bowl and cast up her accounts again after all.

How she felt didn't matter right now, she decided as she paced her bedchamber to try to settle her heaving stomach. If he married her, Zachary would make the best of things for the baby's sake, but one night of unforgettable passion would not sustain a marriage. He hadn't even known who he was making love to at the time, and she had wanted him so badly she had blinded herself to how wrong it was to take what she wanted before she left. She had thought it would cost him nothing, but the stark question was, how could she *not* want him?

She had been so hungry for his loving that night, so desperate for intimacy with him that her cheeks flushed with heat at the thought of all she and Zachary had done to one another. She knew it could never be like that again, even if he did agree to marry her for the sake of the baby. He would feel trapped and resentful and he might not even believe her claim that she thought herself to be barren. But the fact was that his child *was* growing inside her and she gasped a great sigh at the wonder of it, despite all her fears for the future.

She looked much the same as usual by the time she was steady enough for a good look in the watery old mirror she usually only glanced at briefly to make sure she was neat enough to start another day. What on earth would Zachary make of her with this shorn hair? Last time he saw her she had been pampered and painted, and her imitation dark curls had fallen all the way down her back. Now she was plainly and practically dressed in a dark wool gown and her hands were rough with hard work again. She was a little paler than usual but her eyes were brighter, despite the shadows underneath them that even deep sleep didn't seem to wipe out. There were small changes she hoped only she had noticed so far but this child was about to change her whole life and Zachary needed to know about it first. She would have to go to his splendid Flaxonby Hall and ask his butler to take her name in to his master and she would have to stay there until he did so if he tried to turn her away.

She still had a couple of Caro's old visiting cards but it would be yet another lie if she used one to get inside Zachary's home. She sighed. Now she was inventing difficulties before she had even got there, and this had to stop before she told herself it was better to stay away until she was great with child because she would be even more unlikely to be admitted to His Lordship's grand country house if she did that. Resolution made, she packed her best gown and wore her newest cloak and left a letter for her grandparents to say she would be back in a week or so and they were not to worry. If they guessed what the matter was maybe it would be a relief; if not, she would have to tell them when she got back. She felt like a coward for slipping away to catch the stage to Penrith behind their backs; running away without explaining herself felt horribly familiar but she still had to do it.

Chapter Twelve

Martha planned to take the most direct route to the nearest town to Flaxonby Hall but she couldn't stop thinking about Zachary's reaction to her news. And she was hoping he hadn't yet sought comfort in another woman's arms. Even the thought of him making sweet, hot love to a stranger made her heart sink and her head hurt so badly that she was tempted to turn back and just send him a letter. The thought of anyone else opening his mail for him and deciding which letters were worthy of the viscount's personal attention, and which were not, made her feel sick again so that was not an option. Fury nearly outdid her misery at the thought of him being distracted by an elegant and impossibly lovely courtesan, or a fine lady he would be proud to wed in fine style as soon as the dust had settled on his failed nuptials to that showy Lady Fetherall, the fool who had run off with another man rather than marry him.

Martha had missed him so much, had agonised

about what she had done with him so often that she couldn't bear the thought of him moving on with a shrug of his broad shoulders and an *Oh, well*. She sighed and tried not to dwell on the fact that men who had to wed women for the sake of a child were not often faithful to their marriage vows so she might have to get used to being horribly jealous.

Even if he agreed to wed her, she would have no right to demand sole possession of his magnificent body or the noble heart he did his best to hide from the rest of the world. She would break if she let herself love him when he could not love or respect her back after what she had done to him, so she had best make sure she didn't love him. Tears threatened as she dreamed of the marriage she could have had with him if she wasn't such a fool and had accepted his proposal that last night instead of running away. She blinked them back and forbade herself the luxury of loving him. This wasn't a fairy story; this was real life and she had a very real babe growing inside her to whom she owed a lot more than a few impossible dreams.

When the stage stopped for a quick change of horses and a few snatched refreshments, Martha spotted the name Holdfast Village on a waybill. Temptation sneaked in and whispered, *Well, why not go and take a look at it?* She told herself it wasn't cowardice to take a small diversion from the logical route between Greygil and Flaxonby. She hadn't paid for the next stage yet and since she was so close to the place, she might as well go and see what all the fuss had been about. Ten miles wasn't far; she could stay overnight and resume her journey tomorrow. At least this way she would know what she had cost Zachary by making it impossible for him to marry Caro.

In the end, Martha was glad to step down from the swaying coach for a few hours' relief from the nausea of her journey in the lumbering coach. She didn't think she could have endured another mile without casting up her accounts over her fellow passengers, and most of them didn't deserve it. It had been bad enough before the smell of raw onions on a fellow passenger's breath had haunted the rest of them even after he had disembarked. She read the name Holdfast on the next signpost with a sigh of relief. Of course, she wasn't here solely to put off having to go to Flaxonby Hall to ask Zachary to marry her after all. She was here to see the place he had been forced to give up.

It felt so good to wash and run a comb through her still very short hair. She looked like a boy dressed up in his sister's clothes for a bet, she decided with a grimace at her own reflection in the square of mirror provided in the bare but spotless bedchamber at the village inn. If only her own hair would hurry up and grow, she could be rid of the dark ends that were already making the stripe of red underneath look ridiculous. She almost wished Grandmama had done what Martha had wanted her to and shaved it all off when she got home, but she pulled up the hood of her cloak and hoped nobody would look too closely at her.

This inn seemed like the most prosperous place in the village but that wasn't saying much. Martha saw everywhere the proof of how grindingly hard a landlord and employer Tolbourne was. As if she needed another reason to be ashamed of having for a grandfather, he clearly didn't care what anyone thought of him round here. He behaved better at Tolbourne House, where his servants and tenants and workers were housed in basic quarters but not in hovels like these. London was close enough to Tolbourne House to lure everyone away if he paid starvation wages and housed them in such tumbledown old places, she supposed. It felt like a blessing that her married name hid her identity since she might have ended up sleeping in a hedge if they knew she was their hated landlord's kin.

'She must have been sick, though, mustn't she? Wouldn't have had her hair cut close as a lousy urchin if she didn't have to, now would she? Not a nicely spoken lady like her,' she heard the landlord whisper to his wife as she walked very carefully down the highly polished staircase a few moments later because she didn't want to slip and risk harming her still very tiny child.

'There's nowt wrong with her so you stop your fussing. We need the money too bad to turn a respectable widow away from our doors so you stow your noise and get on back to work.'

Martha hid a smile as she heard the innkeeper return to the tap with a few gruff mutters about being under the cat's paw and risks they didn't ought to take and never mind the money.

'I would like to walk in the fresh air after all those hours cooped up in the coach,' Martha said to the landlady as if she hadn't heard his grumbles. 'Hold-fast Castle looked very fine in the distance on our way here so I thought I could take a closer look if you would be so kind as to tell me the best way I can get to it from here.'

'They do say it was a very fine old place once upon a time, ma'am, but there's not much to see up close but ruin and neglect now, I'm afraid. It's a pleasant enough walk I suppose, but don't go expecting too much at the end of it.'

'I promise not to but I do need a walk to blow the cobwebs away and make sure I have an appetite for some dinner tonight.'

'Then take the left turn at the crossroads and stay on the road for a while. There's a path off to your right the village girls used to take when they worked at the castle. It's been worn so deep over the years you can't miss it even now there's no work left up there,' the landlady said with a sad shake of her head at the way things were at Holdfast now.

Wandering along the little-used track a few minutes later, Martha wondered how it must feel for the villagers who had remained here to scratch out a living as best they could while watching the castle fall ever deeper into ruin when it had once been the hub of the whole area. She shook her head at the folly of a spoilt gentleman with nothing better to do than lose the vast fortune his wife had brought to their marriage in games of chance. So much history and ancient power gone in the blink of an eye, she thought, and paused to stare up at the stern old stone towers now only under siege from sapling trees and invading creepers.

It seemed criminal to see this once mighty old place sold out of the family that built it to pay off Zachary's grandfather's debts of so-called honour. No wonder his wife, who'd had no power to stop it slipping out of her hands because everything she owned became her husband's property when she married him, had turned into a bitter woman who had made her son feel that he must strive all the hours God sent to regain her once great heritage. And why didn't Zachary's grandfather think of his wife and child when he was risking everything he had in a silly game?

Zachary had told her that his father had worked like a demon to keep his own estates from the creditors, then saved every penny he could to buy this place back one day. Zachary had only been a boy when he had inherited his father's title and become head of the family, all because his grandfather had been such a fool that he hadn't been able to stop at losing his own shirt; he'd had to lose his wife's as well.

Martha still spared a worryingly tender smile at the thought of *her* Viscount Elderwood shaking his head and arguing that it had done him no harm to grow up fast, but she wasn't so sure. It must have been so hard for that grieving boy to become Viscount Elderwood when he was far too young to worry about old debts and duties. He wasn't the sort to shrug and get on with being a boy until he was ready to be a viscount. She imagined him solemn-eyed and so painfully young as he sat by his dying grandmother's bedside making promises no boy should be asked to make. He would have felt the wrongs his grandfather had done her, shouldered the burden of duty that had ruled his father's life.

Young Zachary's burdens felt like a heavy weight on her own shoulders as she walked ever closer to his grandmother's once grand ancestral home and she thought of the child growing inside her. She hoped he or she never felt the crushing weight of this poor old castle on their shoulders as its father did on his. Of course Zachary was going to decide it was his duty to marry her when he knew about her child, but she didn't want that child to have to carry on the fight for this sad old place one day.

She still had to get into another swaying coach and head for Flaxonby Hall tomorrow. Her child needed a father and Zachary was the best one it could have, but she could face that uncomfortable truth again tomorrow.

Holdfast Castle was finally right in front of her, and every year of Tolbourne's possession was obvious in the broken and missing windows and creeper-covered walls. Brambles and ivy and old-man's-beard were nudging through gaps in ancient shutters and doors, and seedling trees grew on its battlements. It would not be very long before roofs fell in and rain and invading plants broke its mighty walls down so it was truly in ruins.

Staring at her grandfather's wilful neglect of a place he would have bought only for the purpose of exploiting it, she nearly understood why Zachary thought Holdfast was worth marrying a stranger for. There were traces of pleasure gardens and the remnants of a more gracious way of life here, and she was torn between understanding the pride and past glories Zachary's grandmother had clung to so desperately and hating the place that had so nearly blighted his life.

Martha was surprised to see that a little church in the grounds had been neatly maintained. A section of curtain wall was gone but the rest was cared for. Those still working here or on far-flung farms must use it as their parish church, then. She passed through the wicket gate just as the sun came out and it felt like a blessing. It was still shining when she came out again, musing on lives once lived here and Zachary's ancestors who lay inside the church. He would have been the heir of such mighty border lords and ladies if his grandfather had been a better man, and the sight of all that grand history had made her feel even less grand than usual.

Zach bit back a gasp of shock—and maybe even delight—as Mrs Martha Lington emerged from Hold-fast Chapel. He marvelled at her gift for turning up in the most unlikely of places, while he drank in the glorious sight of her from the shadows of the ancient yew trees in the churchyard.

She looked like all his wildest fantasies come true, but then she would, wouldn't she? He had only had fantasies about her ever since the first night they met. This was how she was meant to be, slender and self-contained in her plain dark grey gown and russet cloak. Her hair was very short and he could almost hear her getting frustrated with what was left of it, only a hint of her own bright colour at the roots of it in the spring sunshine. How had he ever mistaken her for her sister even with that dark dye to hide her true colours? He felt like a fool as she looked around her with a puzzled frown, as if she could sense him gaping at her. He didn't want her to think she was being sized up by a villain from the shadows.

'Martha,' he said as he stepped forward.

'Zachary!' she gasped. 'What are you doing here?' she asked. He could see more colour in her cheeks as he closed the gap between them.

'You took the words right out of my mouth,' he said. She sighed as if he was being exasperating and he supposed he was.

'I came to find out why this place was so important that you would agree to a hateful marriage,' she said as if that explained everything.

'And what have you decided?' he asked warily.

'That it's a poor old place and the village isn't much better.' She looked so guilty about it, and he knew she was feeling responsible for her grandfather's ruthlessness, though none of it was her fault.

'The villagers know where the blame lies. You are not responsible for Tolbourne's actions.'

'Only my own,' she said bleakly.

'What harm have you ever done anyone, Mrs Lington?'

'That's not what you said the last time we met.'

'I said a lot of things I shouldn't have that night.'

'Most of them were true,' she said and finally met his eyes with a challenge to deny it. What a contrary woman she was, but he was so glad he'd found her—and at Holdfast, of all places.

'No, most of them were hurt pride,' he replied. Why hadn't he admitted that folly even to himself until now?

'Ah, yes. Viscount Elderwood's lordly pride. It was wounded by the very thought of marriage to a cit's granddaughter, then I came along and made it even worse.'

He felt as if she was building a wall between them and it was his job to knock it down again.

'I'm surprised he hasn't sold it off a piece at a time for building stone,' she carried on doggedly.

'So am I. Now let's stop talking about him and concentrate on you and me.'

'Why?'

'We have unfinished business.'

'Goodness, are you still worrying about that all these weeks later?' she said. But why had she gone so white? 'Do you hate me?' she added wistfully.

'No, of course not. Why would I?' he said, horrified that she thought he might hate her. On the contrary—his heart had leapt and the world seemed painted in brighter colours when he spotted her and realised she was not another dream he was going to wake up from, lonely and frustrated.

'Because I pretended to be Caro and robbed you of your chance to get this poor old place back.'

'You did me a favour, as well as the new Mrs Harmsley and her husband. I know she was with child when Tolbourne forced our betrothal on her.'

'Oh.'

'And before you ask, I would rather live in a hovel on bread and water than wed your sister with another man's child in her belly. Finding out how close we came to disaster made me put Holdfast in its proper place.'

'And what is that?'

'Always second to my family and all the people I love.'

She looked uncomfortable and blushed for some odd reason. 'You must think me a dishonourable woman after what I did.'

'No, I think that you love your half-sister,' he said with a twist of something like sadness in his gut because she didn't love him. 'You would do anything for someone you love, wouldn't you, Mrs Martha Lington?'

'That's not what you said last time we were together either.'

'I was furious with you for lying to me and hurt when you refused to take my proposal seriously.'

'It wasn't a proposal; it was a demand,' she said with a cool stare.

'I did say I was furious, didn't I?'

'So you did,' she said flatly.

'And hurt.'

'Oh, dear, poor Lord Elderwood,' she said. He wasn't sure why she was goading him again but he was tired of tiptoeing around.

'How did you feel when you ran away from me, Martha?' he asked, keeping his gaze on hers in a challenge to avoid the subject yet again.

'Tired,' she said defensively, but he saw the way she firmed her lips and raised her chin before she could hold his gaze. 'And hurt,' she admitted reluctantly.

There was something a lot deeper than hurt in her dark green eyes. 'I'm sorry I hurt you,' he said gently.

'We hurt one another,' she said with a shrug. 'I suppose it was inevitable, given who I really am and who you are.'

'Who am I, then?'

'A viscount, Lord of Flaxonby and master of all you survey.'

'You make me sound like a medieval tyrant.'

'If the cap fits you might as well wear it.'

'It doesn't. I am just a fallible human being, like you and every other being on this earth. I refuse to be defined by my ancestry and so should you.'

'Think who I am, though, Zachary. I was cast off by my own grandfather simply because it suited him not to own up to me.'

'Your mother's parents clearly love and value you and accept you as your father's daughter, though, so why do Tolbourne's lies still matter to you?'

Zach imagined some local bully getting hold of that slander and taunting her with it, and he wanted to go back in time to chase the oaf off and protect her, but time didn't work like that.

'Maybe you're right,' she said, looking astonished.

'Good for me,' he said wryly.

'But you're still a viscount.'

'I blame my parents.'

'Idiot,' she said and almost smiled at long last. He wanted to hug her and a great deal more, but this was not the right time or place.

'Why are you really here, Martha?'

'Why are you?'

'I came here to say goodbye to Holdfast before I came to find you.' He watched her pick through that sentence and waited patiently because she looked almost breakable, and that wasn't the Martha he knew. This version of her was so much thinner and paler and she looked almost haunted, as if she had been trying to forget how bitterly they had parted as well. As if she might even have missed him, if he was really going to get his hopes up.

'Why would you do that?' she asked carefully, and he tried not to be disappointed.

He hadn't even known for sure that was what he was going to do until he saw her emerge from the chapel. His delight at seeing her had told him he hadn't come north to make his peace with Mr and Mrs Harmsley and bid goodbye to this sad old dream, after all; he really had come to find her.

'Because we have some very unfinished business, and you know it.'

'Why? Why are you so determined to wed me, my lord? I told you I could not bear you a child, so why can it matter to you what I do or where I go?'

She looked as if this was the burning question she had been longing to ask him, and he wasn't quite ready to answer it yet.

'Because deep down there was always a part of me that knew you were you and not your sister. The first moment I saw you on the stairs, my opinion of my bride-to-be flipped upside down and I discovered I was actually looking forward to our wedding night.'

'There was no wedding,' she pointed out coolly.

'Then marry me now. We can find out everything we need to about one another at our leisure and pleasure. So please will you marry me this time, Martha?'

'Why?'

Why? What sort of question was that? He felt as if all the air had been sucked out of his lungs as he pulled in a great breath. *Because she needs to, of course*, he told himself. He saw her rub her midriff and wondered if she too was feeling the emptiness of a future without a child, and the lack of urgency of a wedding between them. Then she did it again and he was certain she didn't know she was doing it because not even her sadness at her lack of a child could explain the way she was stroking her flat belly as if she was trying to make sure her agitation did no harm in there.

He felt his heartbeat jar as the idea that he could have got her with child after all occurred to him. Wild hope threatened to make him clumsy with her yet again, and he bit back a knot of hasty questions as she dropped her hand the instant she realised what she was doing. She looked so conscious and guilty, and as sharp desire and so many complicated feelings threatened to sweep over him, he knew he must be patient and not jump to conclusions without good reason.

He made himself remember her painfully honest confession after they had made love and he had realised who she was. She had been so sure she was barren, so how likely was it that he had got her with child in one passionate session of heady lovemaking? Yet he still saw a burn of hot colour on her previously pallid cheeks, and now she was staring at anything but him again while he tried to keep hold of his hopes and not feel as if the whole world was changing around him.

'You haven't told me why you came this far from your home when you must be busy getting ready for the lambing season,' he said almost casually.

'No, I haven't, have I?' she agreed with a sigh. 'I did want to know why this place mattered so much that you would have sacrificed your freedom and self-respect for it.'

'And…?' he said, holding his breath as he watched her struggle for words.

'Then I was coming to find you,' she admitted with a gasp for air that said it was a mighty effort for her to admit it out loud. 'I came here first to find out why you nearly broke yourself to possess it.'

'I wasn't the one who was lying.'

'To love and to cherish from this day forward?' she prompted, quoting part of the marriage service at him and raising her eyebrows.

'I'm not sure I could have said that to your half-sister, even if you hadn't jumped in to save her. I hope guilt and common sense would have choked the words off.'

'Maybe they would have,' she said, looking unconvinced.

'And if your sister had been there to marry me, I would never have met you and had my life turned upside down.'

'Poor Lord Elderwood,' she said, with enough irony to make him look deeper into the contrary emotions making her eyes seem even darker than usual.

'I never *wanted* to marry her,' he added.

'But you still promised to.'

'Well, she seemed to want to marry me and at the time I wanted this place badly enough to oblige her.'

'She could have given it you if you had married her.'

'It would have cost us both too much, even if she hadn't been in love with another man. But I know a diversion when I hear one, so why were you going to find me, Martha?'

She flinched and turned away, seemed to search for a place to sit, then plumped down on an ancient oak seat in the chapel porch as if her legs refused to hold her up any longer. He followed her in and took the one opposite so she would have to look at him. She cunningly avoided his eyes by staring instead at the flagstones worn down by generations of worshippers. 'I have to—' she began, then broke off.

'What do you have to do, Martha?' he prompted gently, although his heart was racing again with wild hope and nearly as much fear that he was wrong.

'I have to—' She broke off again and looked so frustrated and self-conscious that he wanted to lean forward and kiss her, but they were in the doorway of a chapel and he was much too impatient to know if he was right.

'Best say whatever it is so we can deal with it together,' he advised gruffly and held his breath when she sighed and looked haunted.

'I think I am with child,' she announced in such a hurry that the words almost tumbled into one another. 'There,' she added before he could even find breath to speak past the importance and shock and pride of knowing he was right, and wasn't it wondrous that he was going to become a father in the autumn? 'You're horrified to hear it, aren't you, Zachary? I knew you would be. I should have written to tell you about my suspicions so you could at least have had time to come to terms with the idea and decide what to do about it without me sitting here waiting to find out what you want to do about us. It seemed too personal to put in a letter and send by mail when it could have been broken open or even got lost altogether. What would you think of me if my secret came out before you knew about it and had the chance to decide what you should do?'

'Stop!' he exclaimed and despite his suspicions the shock of having them confirmed made him sound harsh. He saw her flinch and was horrified to see the mother of his unborn child looking frightened of him when he would rather die than hurt her. 'Just stop talking for a moment, Martha,' he said more gently and reached across the gap between them to take her hands in his and stop her twining her fingers together so frantically it must hurt. 'Don't say another word until you have caught your breath and given me a chance to catch mine.'

'You don't—'

This time he stopped her with a finger on her trembling lips. He gentled his touch until it was a caress. How he had longed to feel her mouth against his bare skin these last few endless weeks. Why the devil hadn't he given in to that longing and come to find her before?

'I told you how much I want to marry you the night you ran away from me, and I repeated that desire just a moment ago, but I want it even more now, my Martha. It feels as if you are holding the rest of my life in your hands.'

'You didn't say you *wanted* to marry me that night. You felt obliged to offer for me after everything we did together and it looked like the last thing you wanted to do when you were so furious with me.'

'I was furious because you had deceived me and didn't tell me so before we became lovers; you are right about that much of what I said that night. Do you really think you can get inside my head as well as under my skin and know everything I think and feel for you from one outraged outburst? Is that really all you thought we were that night, Martha, just four legs in a bed? If so, you have no idea how magnificent that night felt for me.

'You're right; I *was* determined to marry the Lady Fetherall I thought I was making love to, before I knew I had been royally hoodwinked by the Tolbourne sisters. I began that week determined never to lay a finger on your sister with passionate intent but ended it yearning for our marriage to start because I would be marrying you and not her, if that makes any sense at all. You know as well as I do that marriage is the right thing for both of us now. Just promise me you will turn up to marry me this time, Martha? If not for my sake or yours, please say you'll do it for our baby?'

'But you could do so much better than me, Zachary. My sister could have brought you all this and most of the money you would need to set it right as well. Tolbourne was so desperate for her to marry a lord he would have paid over half his fortune if you had only held out for it.'

'Blood money,' he said shortly. 'Can't you just say yes to me for once in your life, Martha? It's not only about us now. We have to think of our child, even if you don't want to marry me for my own sake.'

'Do you think I have been able to do anything else but think of you ever since I left you that night in

Kent? Of course I have to think about the baby too and what all this means,' she said with an impatient wave at her slender person as if he ought to know what she was talking about.

'All what? You look as if you have lost weight rather than gaining any.'

'I can't help it; I keep being sick,' she admitted with a furious, frustrated frown. 'I need to eat for two, but even the thought of food nauseates me at certain times of the day and I can't face it. I only want to do my best for our child, Zachary, really I do, but it's not been a very good best so far, I'm afraid.'

She sounded as if she had spent more time worrying about the welfare of their child than her unwed status and that felt so typical of her that it pinched at his heart. Of course he wanted this unique woman to be the mother of his children and no other, but he also wanted her for her own sake as well. How was he ever going to convince her of it now?

'I know you will always do your best for the child, and when you stop agonising about the future maybe our baby will settle down of its own accord, particularly when you begin to look after yourself better and I'm with you all the time to make sure that you do.' He stopped and ran a distracted hand through his already windswept hair. '*Our* baby,' he said unsteadily. 'You're carrying our baby, Martha. Only think of it!'

'I am. Everyone will say I trapped you and I'm not at all the sort of wife a viscount should marry. I feel as if I'm forcing you into marriage every bit as surely as Tolbourne tried to force you to marry my sister for the sake of this poor old castle.'

'Don't even think it,' he said. The thought of his engagement to the wrong sister made *him* feel nauseous. 'And why won't they say *I* trapped *you*? You are so beautiful and so well worth trapping and exactly the sort of bride a sensible Yorkshire landowner would choose. I hear tell that what you don't know about sheep isn't worth knowing, and I know your mother's family can trace their line back to Scottish lairds as well as Saxon earls. My mother will approve of you as my bride even more when she hears about that part of your lineage.'

'Why would she approve of me? She must have been ashamed of you having to marry Caro for the castle, since none of your family came to watch you marry her. I know they disapprove of us Tolbourne girls so please don't try to pretend they don't.'

'Not you, him. And my mother will approve of you, first of all because you're not your sister, and then because you're carrying my child. She's a proud Scot so she'll be delighted your Winton grandfather has good clan blood in his veins to water down the rest of our poor Sassenach variety. Of course she's going to approve of you, Martha, and why on earth would she not? You are a gentlewoman descended from earls and lairds who were men of power when my ancestors were still sweeping floors and digging ditches.'

'If they ever did so I'm sure they did it with style.'

'I'm not sure you can dig a ditch with style, but

never mind my ancestors. You are not my equal, Martha, but my superior in birth and in history. Your Winton grandparents could decide *I'm* unworthy of *you*. Even if they give their consent, I dare say they will only tolerate me for your sake and for their great-grandchild's.'

'Ancient nobility doesn't put food on the table or coal on the range,' she argued with a faint smile at his argument. 'Nor does it change the fact that my paternal grandfather had me legally declared a bastard. That's a very good reason why you should not marry me, even with your child growing inside me.'

'No, it's the silliest one you have come up with so far. We both know Tolbourne's slur on your mother was nothing but a self-serving lie. You are so like your half-sister, apart from your glorious red hair, that you two would only have to stand side by side to make it obvious to anyone who looked at you that you must share a father. He can hardly claim otherwise now you have fooled him and all the rest of us that you were your half-sister for an entire week and not one of those present suspected otherwise.'

Zach paused and hoped that indisputable fact convinced her. The *ton* were openly mocking Tolbourne's claim that his elder granddaughter was not his son's child now that it was so obviously a lie.

'I know your maternal grandparents would still love you even if it were true.'

'You seem to know a lot about me.'

'I made it my business to after you left. I knew I needed to protect you and your sister from Tolbourne's fury so I dug through his past for more secrets. Nothing of what I found out reflects well on him. His cruel lie about your red hair making you a bastard says more about him than it ever did about you.'

'Grandfather Winton's little sister had bright red hair,' she said with a self-conscious smoothing of her shorn locks that had the same brightness beginning to show through. 'She died in infancy so there is no portrait of her to prove it, only Grandpapa's word, and the judge chose not to accept it.'

'Then we will find a lawyer who will make a judge listen if you want your legitimacy made official. I suspect Tolbourne will be so delighted when you and I wed that he'll withdraw his slander on your late mother without even being asked to.'

'That's almost a good reason for us *not* to marry, my lord.'

'Almost? You do mean to marry me, then?'

'I don't think I have much choice, Zachary, so long as you're sure that you want me to?'

'Of course I'm sure. I was sure when you came to my room that night and I knew I couldn't let you say whatever you had come to say because I wanted you beyond reason and thought you had come to say you couldn't marry me.'

'I had come to say just that. But despite believing I had come to break off the engagement, you made love to me anyway?'

'You have honest eyes, even when your delicious

mouth is arguing with them, and I read your good-bye in them. I had to stop you saying it somehow.'

'So you kissed me, and one thing led to another.'

'As it always will with us. As it probably would right now if you didn't look so fragile. I fear you might break if I let what I really feel about you and our baby out of its cage.'

'I won't break. I have not been downtrodden all my life like my sister was until she met her husband. I was raised by good people, loved by good people, and I am a strong woman,' she told him.

'Are you indeed?' he asked softly and used their joined hands to raise her to her feet. He met her fascinating eyes with a long, hot look and outlined her lips with his finger again, silently promising her all the things they could share again as soon as he had got his wedding ring on her finger. 'Say you will marry me,' he urged her and let the heat and frustration and need he was struggling with show in a long, hungry look that should tell her he wasn't going to be fobbed off with maybes.

'Why?'

'To make it into a promise of course, so I can trust you not to run away again. Just promise me you really are going to marry me this time, Martha, please?'

'Yes,' she said at last. 'Yes, I will.'

'At last.' He let out a long sigh. He felt as if he had climbed a mountain since he saw her step out of this church porch and could hardly believe his eyes.

'Thank you,' he said, and the tension tightening every muscle and sinew with dread that she might yet refuse him, loosened its hold. It didn't fade completely and it probably would not until he had his ring on her finger and all the right words said at the right time. After waking up that morning and finding his lover had flown without a parting word, he wasn't going to believe she was really going to marry him until she had actually done it.

'I will send for the chaise and four so I can get you home in a lot more comfort than you came here in. Then we can get on with being man and wife as quickly as possible and give this little one the best start in life we can,' he said, and this time he could lay a wondering hand on her still flat belly and make it a solemn vow to all three of them.

Chapter Thirteen

It was obvious; Zachary wanted to give his future child as much respectability as they could get for it. If this was a boy, then her son would be heir to a fine title and most of Zachary's wealth and possessions. As many months as could be got between his parents' marriage and his birth would feel very important to both father and son but what if the baby was a girl? Would Zachary decide she hadn't been worth the trouble? He might wish he had held out for a more suitable mother for his children and paid Martha off. She shook her head at the slowly passing countryside outside the carriage window and told herself to stop having all these silly doubts before she ruined her second marriage before it had even begun.

She had never thought she would have a second marriage. It had felt as if she must walk on alone for the rest of her life when Tom was killed, and now here she was, on the way back to Greygil with her soon-to-be second husband riding alongside the carriage and so protective of her and their unborn child. She didn't feel much like sturdy Widow Lington. She wondered how she was going to cope with being someone so very different from that busy country-woman. It felt so strange for her to be about to start a new life as the next Lady Elderwood.

Whatever would Tom think of her if he could see her now? Would he feel betrayed because she had made love with Zachary that night for no other reason than because she desperately wanted to? Or would he be glad she was not going to be lonely for the rest of her life after all? The latter of course, because he had truly loved her. Tom would never have wanted her to live without happiness or companion-ship for the rest of her life.

Zachary Chilton was a good man too, a gentleman in every sense of the word. He would never make his wife feel 'less than him.' She knew he was always going to do his best to make her feel secure and val-ued as his wife and the mother of his children. She was not at all sure his family would agree with him, or ever truly accept her, despite what he had said about his mother.

Oh, dear, here I go again, making a catastro-phe out of my future life before it's even started, she thought.

She only needed to worry about Zachary and their child now. Never mind what a pack of stuffy aris-tocrats thought of them. She would be his wife in a few days' time and that was all that really mattered.

I am carrying Viscount Elderwood's child, she

thought dreamily, and watched him waiting for the carriage at the side of the road to make sure all was well with her.

She waved and smiled to say, yes, this journey was very much better than her last one, thank you. He looked more boyish and eager than she had ever seen him before, now that they were engaged to be married as soon as possible. How could she resist him when he was so protective and apparently delighted with her and his unborn child?

The awful truth was she couldn't resist him anyway. He had made her pulse race from the first moment she set eyes on him. He only had to enter a room or pass an open door for her to feel as if everything in her world had suddenly grown brighter and more alive. Now she was going to marry him. It would be hard to keep her passion for him a secret but she would have to try.

It felt better not to look too deeply into this new life she was about to make with Zachary and their child. She could watch out for Zachary riding ahead and indulge in a fantasy that their marriage would grow into a love match, given enough time and if they both worked at it. He had told her he must ride because he wasn't to be trusted in a carriage with her and she didn't deserve to be pawed by an overeager lover whilst she was fighting the nausea he had caused in the first place. It seemed like a promising start, if he meant it. He seemed so proud of himself for causing her nausea that she didn't point out that the cause had been very much a joint effort. She had enjoyed every second of making this baby with him and now she needed to put the tiny little life they had made between them first and forget her doubts and fears for all their sakes so they could make a good marriage.

Apparently content that it was safe for them to continue for a few more miles before he insisted they must stop so she could rest and refresh herself, Zachary urged his mighty stallion back into the steady trot the fiery animal looked so bored by that Martha almost laughed. Now she could look out for the occasional glimpse of her future husband's broad shoulders, strong back and narrow hips and his long, strong legs. She would try her best not to long for more than he wanted this marriage to be. Pining for the impassioned lover he had been at Tolbourne House would only make her a disappointed woman. Yet it was so hard not to dream of more as she watched the road ahead for her sternly handsome Viking lord, with nothing else to do but dream about him and the family they were already making.

'At least I found you an excellent papa,' she muttered to her still very tiny baby and was glad she had refused Zach's offer to find her a maid to accompany her home so she would have feminine company along the way and not need to look after herself. As if she wasn't used to doing so, she silently chided her overprotective husband-to-be. She had never been wrapped in cotton wool as his sisters would have been, but she supposed she must learn to be a lady of leisure. When she wasn't waiting to become a mother, what did a viscountess do with herself all day? It was an active not a passive role, though, wasn't it, being a mother?

And the world would soon find out that Lord and Lady Elderwood had not sat politely on their hands until they married one another with indecent haste. The gossips would be delightfully scandalised when her pregnancy began to show. Well, sooner or later Martha would have to consider Zachary's consequence and give in to the role she was about to play in his life, but she was so glad she had managed to avoid having a maidservant thrust upon her for now. She didn't want a stranger knowing she was enceinte before the wedding, and if that made her a fool then so be it.

'I am going to be Lady Elderwood as well as your mama, baby,' she told herself as much as her future child.

Oh, so you're the new Viscountess Elderwood, are you? Well, how d'you do, madam? Thought you was marryin' the dark-haired one, not a chestnut mare, Chilton.

Oh, dear. Martha sighed, and tried not to think what Zachary's friends were really going to say about her behind his back.

'Martha Louisa Chilton at your service, my lord,' she whispered to Zachary's back as she caught sight of him riding around the next bend ahead of the carriage, and felt her heartbeat race with excitement yet again despite all her stern orders for it not to bother.

'It sounds so much easier to live up to, and not

so very different from Martha Louisa Lington if I don't think about it too hard,' she added to pretend her conversation with herself was too important to be interrupted by glimpses of Zachary's powerful figure up ahead and all the things she would like to do with him if he wasn't so worried about her and the child.

'If only you loved me, what a wonderful new adventure this would be, Zachary,' she whispered to the wood and glass between her and her next sighting of him. She had to strain for a glimpse of him through the window of the splendid travelling chaise she knew he must have ordered for Caro's use after their marriage. If anything could bring her back down to earth with a thump, it was the thought of what might have happened if she had turned down Caro's plea for help.

'I will just have to get used to not seeing him, not being with him all the time. A viscountess can't cling on to her viscount's coattails. I promise not to cling to you when you need to be free to live your own life either, my little love,' she told the child inside her.

She feared how hard that promise might be to keep when she already loved it so dearly, but at least that vow was a couple of decades away from being called on. Hopefully there would be more children to stop her being lonely Lady Elderwood, who sat about dreaming of impossible things all day—a husband who loved her, a family she could be at the heart of instead of on the just-about-acceptable edges, a lover so eager and powerful they could reshape the whole idea of aristocratic marriage together and make it fashionable to adore and want your own spouse instead of someone else's. Even to her it sounded impossible, so she had best be plain old Martha Louisa and find her own happiness in this coming child and the prospect of marrying such an honourable husband.

Zach thought three days should be plenty of time to get married, but in the end it took a week to marry Martha. Everyone insisted that one week was the bare minimum he must wait, and at least it gave his close family time to get to Cumberland as fast as a messenger could ride to Flaxonby and tell them he really was getting wed this time and they must get here to support him as fast as possible.

Who he was marrying must have come as a shock, but they still came in a hurry and arrived with almost a day to spare. They couldn't hate the idea of him marrying Martha as much as they had the idea of him marrying Caroline, then. Zach wasn't sure it was altogether a good thing that they approved when his family arrived in force and his mother brought the family wedding veil and *her* mother's diamond tiara for Martha to wear, as well as both of his sisters to be bridesmaids and his brother. Max would be groomsman.

It wasn't that he didn't love his family, and of course he wanted them to be here on the most important day of his life so far, but his mother was a force to be reckoned with and his eldest sister had taken most of her cues from her mother. He didn't want

Martha to feel overwhelmed by the Dowager Viscountess Elderwood and the Honourable Mrs Breen, both of them decked out in full battle order. He could imagine her eyeing them warily and wondering if she was expected to be that stiff and dignified in future.

Heaven forbid, he thought with a shudder at the very idea of his Martha ever being so stately and constrained. He liked her as she was, her freedom of movement and impulsiveness and fiery spirit and most of all, her independent nature. He didn't want her to ape her future mother-in-law and eldest sister-in-law. He wanted her just as she was and as soon as possible, he recalled as he concentrated on his wife-to-be instead of the rest of his family and sighed at the interminable time it was taking for this morning to be over so he could get on with marrying Martha.

'I am never going to get married,' Max told him almost seriously as he watched Zach pacing the room like a caged tiger.

Zach was lucky to be staying in one of Squire Winton's wealthier neighbours' guest bedchambers rather than the local inn, so he had plenty of room to pace, but every minute he had to wait for his wedding felt like an hour. He frowned at his brother's announcement and wondered if Max was trying to divert him from his nerves and impatience or warn him that the Chilton succession would rest solely on his own shoulders. The thought of his coming child was the antidote he needed against worrying about how various parts of his family would greet his new wife. They would just have to learn that she and their child came first with him now. For so long he had felt as if his brother and younger sister, Becky, were his responsibility. Neither of them could remember their father very well so of course he would still try to guard and guide them as best he could, but he wasn't their father. Time he stepped back and let them live their lives and make mistakes.

Max was twenty and Becky seventeen so she would make her social debut next season. Zach would just have to keep his fingers crossed they didn't share their grandfather's mania for the card tables along with his careless elegance and easy charm. By next spring he would be a doting papa, God willing, and too far away to keep a hawk eye on Becky and her hopeful suitors. Maybe Max would do it for him, which reminded him that they were speaking of his brother's thoughts on marriage.

'What sensible female would have you?' he replied easily enough. Once he would have worried why Max was so sure he wasn't going to do this. Maybe his little brother had been disappointed in love, but he was still plenty young enough to meet the right woman and change his mind. Max would want to marry her when he did, would need to walk with her at his side for the rest of his life, and he wouldn't feel trapped by marriage but liberated by it, almost newly made.

Zach frowned as he wondered how Martha felt about being his bride. Did she feel trapped by their marriage? He hoped not and silently swore to make it as easy on her as he could. He still didn't know exactly how she felt about him, but he knew this was unlike her first marriage. He didn't even want to think about how she had felt on the morning of her wedding to Lington. He knew she was nervous about *this* wedding and his family, and that she must be missing her sister.

Mrs Harmsley said she was too close to her confinement now to make it a good idea for her to travel. Zach respected her tact and would be grateful forever that she had found the courage to flee with her lover rather than marrying him. He felt empty and cold at the thought of the gaping absence in his life if he had never met Martha. She was the most vivid, stubborn and complicated woman he had ever met and he could never imagine being bored in her company. His smiled at the thought of her being fussed over and feeling impatient and frustrated at this very moment, and their marriage felt like an adventure he couldn't wait to begin.

That reminded him, how many minutes had passed since he last wondered how long he must wait for them to be man and wife? He glanced at his watch again and found out that a man could think about a great deal in a short time. He sighed and wished the minutes would hurry up and pass instead of limping along so slowly.

'What were we talking about?' he asked his brother absently.

'Brides.'

'Ah, yes,' he replied, and dreamed about his again until his smile had quite a lot of wolf in it.

'As I don't want one myself, I won't be taking any

lessons from you,' his brother interrupted again. 'Although your bride does seem a very fine lady, and if I *were* a marrying man I might cut you out and run away with her,' Max added blithely.

Zach could hardly hit his brother on his wedding day, but even the thought of Max trying to act like Young Lochinvar with his Martha made his fingers curl into fists. But he loved his brother, even when he was being recklessly provoking.

'You only met her last night and she's marrying me in—' as calmly as he could Zach straightened out his clenched fingers so he could check his watch yet again '—half an hour,' he said, and held it up to his ear so he could hear it tick and make sure the damned thing was still working.

'If you survive that long,' Max said with a highly amused look at Zach's tense face. 'If not. I will just have to step in and keep her and her little Chilton-to-be in the family.'

'I told you that in confidence,' Zach gritted out and had to fight the urge to thump his own brother once again. He knew very well Max was trying to divert him from the way time had slowed to a snail's pace.

'I wish I could have been a fly on the wall to watch you being led up the garden path by my clever future sister-in-law while she pretended to be her half-sister and you thought you were about to marry the wrong one.'

'You should be glad you're not, since I would have to swat you.'

'Very messy and not very brotherly either.'

'Yet so satisfying, so best be glad you were *not* there and I saw her first because I would have fought for her, little brother—never doubt it.'

'After you had seen her sister first and decided you didn't want to fight for her,' Max teased to try to stop Zach pacing the floor.

Zach felt savage at the thought of Max lusting after Martha, and what did that say about him? It said he was jealous and possessive and the sooner he got to his wedding night so he and Martha could slake a little of this unruly passion together the better. Not too much, not with her being in a delicate condition, and heaven send him enough restraint to be gentle with her on their wedding night after two months of this endless frustration. He had been an idiot not to chase after her straight away and persuade her he wanted her whether she was with child or not. Now she seemed to think he was only marrying her because she was enceinte. Why didn't she realise she was at the centre of his world?

'Never mind Martha's sister. It's Martha I need and want and Martha I'll be marrying in…' he began, about to check his watch yet again when Max snatched it away.

'I'll tell you when it's time for us to walk to the church.'

'Should have ordered a carriage,' Zach muttered as he wondered what Martha and her grandmother, and every female she had ever met so far as he could tell, were doing at her home right now. Had she been sick this morning? Had any of those fussing females guessed why she was marrying him in such a hurry? Her grandparents had been told, and he knew he was still only on approval as their next grandson-in-law, despite his title and Flaxonby and generations of warrior Chiltons and DeMaynes at his back. He had got their beloved granddaughter with child out of wedlock so he could hardly blame them for that. He still squirmed at the memory of how ignoble and unworthy of her and her baby they had made him feel when he asked them for her hand in marriage and confessed his sins at the same time.

'The church is hardly a hundred yards away,' Max pointed out. What was his brother talking about now?

Oh, yes, a carriage and the church so close to the grandest house in the village, whose owners had insisted the brothers stay there until Zach's wedding to Squire Winton's granddaughter. 'Is it time to go yet?'

'Only if you plan to walk backwards around the village for ten minutes to give at least some of the wedding guests time to arrive before we do, Romeo.'

'Don't. It might be unlucky. I don't want to be a star-crossed lover.'

'No, you want to be a lover full stop. Don't think I haven't noticed how much you want your bride-to-be, Zach. I may be near on a decade younger than you are, but I'm not blind or daft.'

'Not that much younger; I'm only seven and twenty.'

'Poor old man,' Max said, shaking his head as if he pitied Zach. But Zach didn't feel in the least bit pitiable today, or at least he wouldn't once he had got his ring safely on Martha's finger.

He felt proud and nervous and conscious of how seriously he was going to take the vows he was about to make her. And yes, Max was right, he was as randy as a stag in rut. Time he got that part of him under stern control so he didn't disgrace Martha at the wedding or want her immoderately before bedtime. By then he felt he could be excused for wanting her this badly. It was nearly two months since they had made love and there was still no sign of their baby on her slender body, although he had already got used to the sight of her fighting the nausea she could suffer at any time of day.

He frowned at nothing again and hoped she was bearing up and all that fussing wasn't making things worse. He managed to while away a few moments by dreamily wondering when their child would start to show and how soon he would be able to feel it move in her belly after it quickened. He felt besotted and bewildered with the hope and suddenness and responsibility of being a father in a few short months as well as Martha's new husband.

'Poor old man nothing. One day you'll learn better, Max. You'll meet your fate when you least expect to and I'll be waiting to laugh at you for being fool enough to think you could evade it when you do.'

'I know trouble when I see it coming and I can run faster than you,' Max said, as if he really believed life was that easy. Maybe it was for him right now.

'One day you won't want to run,' Zach told him.

He wanted to run *towards* his fate as soon as possible and truly hoped his brother would find a woman he could… Hmm… What *did* he feel for Martha?

'Pah! I shall always run. That's where we're different.'

'I doubt it,' Zach said absently as he wrestled with the problem of what he felt about the woman who was shortly going to be his wife. He really should find out what the answer to that question was before he met her at the altar rail. ·

Chapter Fourteen

'I'm not sure if your mother will ever get over the shock of seeing my shorn head for the first time,' Martha whispered to her brand-new husband as they walked out into the hazy spring sunshine after the wedding.

'I'm not sure *I* shall ever get over the shock of seeing you as you really are for the first time either and realising how thoroughly I had been bamboozled.'

'Not that sort of hair,' she whispered very softly. At least it made her look the picture of a blushing bride as they stood amongst their chattering wedding guests after his teasing reference to their last lovemaking.

'But I like it. I like it a lot,' Zach said, deciding he preferred her flustered and blushing at his audacity to how she was when she walked up the aisle towards him on her grandfather's arm looking so pale he thought she was about to faint. He had wanted to rush towards her instead of dutifully waiting for his bride to join him at the chancel steps.

He had held his breath during every step of her walk up the aisle and forgotten his own nerves in his anxiety about hers. Then he forgot there was anyone else in the church while they made their vows. He made his with heartfelt sincerity, waiting for each one of hers with a sickening jangle of nerves and sheer terror whenever she hesitated or barely seemed able to get the words out. Now he only had to get her away from the wedding breakfast without her fainting or looking so pale that there must be even more suspicion over the urgency of this wedding before the cause became obvious. He wanted Martha to have a happy second wedding day, even if he couldn't give her the time to become properly used to the idea of being his viscountess beforehand.

'That's not fair,' she said gruffly.

'No, it's red.'

'Don't!' she exclaimed, but at least she was smiling, even if it was a resigned, wifely sort of smile because he was being outrageous.

He decided he liked the look of a wifely smile on her face, loved the fact that she was clinging to his arm as if he were her only sure support in an unsteady world. He had better get her with child as often as he dared risk her to the dangers of childbed, since he knew she was only smiling at him like that because she felt fragile and the cause would not show for a few months yet. Until then everyone could think she was merely deeply devoted to her impulsive, impassioned husband with his blessing.

'Married and fathoms deep in love before he gave

her feet time to touch the ground,' he heard somebody whisper sentimentally, and how he wished it were true.

He wondered how many husbands realised they had fallen head over heels in love with their wife at the very moment they were marrying her. Because of course he was. He recalled the moment he had promised to love and cherish her until death did them part and suddenly he knew it was the absolutely truth. It felt like a huge undertaking, marrying this woman who thought he was only being honourable and taking responsibility for his child, when there was so much more to it than that. He still had to persuade her to agree with him, though. There was no point in him blurting it out and expecting her to be delighted. It would be damnably difficult for him to get past three years of blissfully happy marriage with her childhood sweetheart and push *his* way into Lington's sacred space in her heart. And why would she even think about loving the rogue who had got her with child out of wedlock? He couldn't let himself believe in the answer that she would not. It was too bleak.

So he daydreamed about her fiery response to him that night in Kent instead and told himself she must have felt more for him even then than she would let herself admit for it to have happened in the first place, and for it to have been so wild and unrestrained a lovemaking. He hadn't even known her true name at the time, he recalled with a worryingly dreamy smile. Now he was eager to repeat their antics of that night as soon as possible. He couldn't afford to be a dreamer when he needed to court his own wife so well she might even decide to love him back. At the moment, any sign he was turning into her besotted lover would probably be greeted with exasperated bewilderment, and they did have a child to think about.

Martha was his wife! Zach lingered over the wonder of that word for a self-indulgent moment. It would be his privilege to make love to her so tenderly that she would trust him with more of herself than she had so far. He knew she had a yearning heart under the wary looks she often gave him, as if she were expecting him to turn into the stiffly hostile Lord Elderwood he had been that first night at any moment. It might be an uphill battle to convince her that he thought her the finest, most desirable lady in the land, but Zach was going to put all his best efforts into wooing his wife.

Zachary kept her close to his side for the rest of the afternoon and Martha loved the feel of his strong arm around her waist as they talked to their wedding guests. She was touched by his grimace when he had to let her go to drive them slowly up the hill in his flower-bedecked curricle so they had time to greet their well-wishers on the way up to Greygil from the church. He had refused to let her walk and she hadn't even wanted to argue with him today, but he had better not get used to it.

Greygil had never looked lovelier than it did now

she knew she had to quit it for Zach's much grander home. Of course she would have to make a life in Yorkshire with him, but nowhere would ever feel so much like home as this rambling old manor house where she had spent most of her life.

Zach drew rein at the rarely used front door and the sight of it standing open for them made stupid tears stand in her eyes. She blinked them back and smiled a slightly wobbly smile as her new brother-in-law ran up behind them to hold the horses' heads with a graceful bow and impudent look at his new sister-in-law to make her laugh.

'No, Zachary, you mustn't,' she protested when her husband helped her out of the graceful little vehicle then bent to lift her in his arms.

'I already have, my lady,' he told her without even a hitch in his breathing. 'It's not my threshold, but any excuse to hold you is better than none so I expect your grandfather will forgive me,' he told her. She liked this light-hearted, joyful version of the serious, sternly dutiful lord she first met in Kent so she didn't bother to argue with him and felt breathless and feminine and swept off her feet as he lifted her as if she weighed nothing.

'I think he already has,' she whispered in his ear, although he had told her Max knew she was carrying his child. 'You must have convinced him you mean to hold me as often as possible from now on because he was so proud to give me away to you this afternoon, Zachary. I wondered if we were both going to end up in tears when he took my hand to give it to you. You are a brave man to take on such a watering pot as I seem to have become lately.'

'No, but I know I'm a lucky one,' he told her huskily as he paused in the wide doorway to give her a passionate kiss.

Silenced and quite certain she could not stand up on her own if he did try to put her down now, she was glad when he gently set her back on her feet. But he kept his arm around her waist again, despite Max's comically raised eyebrows and the sceptical look the Dowager Lady Elderwood gave them when she was ushered into the room. Martha was so proud of her grandparents for being the gracious hosts of her second wedding, and even Lady Elderwood and her eldest daughter seemed to unbend a little when Squire Winton made a witty speech to welcome his new son-in-law into the family. Clearly the dowager viscountess believed he was joking when he threatened to horsewhip Zachary if he didn't make his granddaughter very happy indeed. Martha wondered if Zachary would take offence at the threat underlying the humour, but when she looked into his fascinating silver-blue eyes, the warmth in them was so irresistible she forgot what she was silently asking him and smiled blissfully back at him.

'I will,' he muttered for her ears only and she had to search her scattered thoughts for his meaning.

Make her happy, of course—that was it. She felt so warm and wanted that she believed him. She *would* be happy as long as she didn't expect too much. If only she could learn to be content with him wanting and maybe even needing his wife until she got too large for him to even find her waist, let alone put his arm around it.

'It will be my absolute pleasure,' he added with a heat in his gaze she would be a naive fool to mistake for anything but his fervent desire for the pleasure they could give one another as soon as they were private together again. She recalled every move and the sweet, hot urgency of making love with him last time and could hardly wait for tonight and all the lovely privacy a newlywed couple were entitled to expect. 'How soon can I begin?' he whispered in her ear.

'You already have,' she murmured and hoped nobody else noticed his arm was around her waist again but this time his hand was flat on the place where his child was growing so secretly only its parents and a few select people knew it was there. Her breath caught at the pride and sensual promise in his gentle touch. Heat swept through her and finally banished the nausea she had been struggling with all day. Excitement and nerves, her grandmother had said when she sent everyone else out of Martha's bedchamber and made her lie quietly on the bed with a cloth soaked in lavender on her forehead until she was well enough to face her own wedding day. Now she wanted this part of it over so urgently that she wriggled in her chair against the wild heat building so relentlessly inside her.

'Please,' she murmured and wasn't even sure what she was asking for as the same frustration and fierce heat blazed back at her from his ice blue eyes and she felt that roaring for far more than just words building ever hotter inside her.

'Time you two lovebirds changed out of your wedding day finery, if you really intend to get wherever you are going to spend the wedding night in time for your dinner,' Max murmured, as if he had seen and understood their urgent glances and thought he should do something about it before everyone else did so as well.

'You promise to be the finest and most tactful of brothers-in-law, dear Maxwell,' Martha murmured back.

'Only if you agree never to call me that again, Lady Elderwood,' he replied, and she jumped at the realisation that really was her name now.

'So long as you call me Martha,' she told him and saw Zachary frown at their byplay and wondered which bit caused it.

'You are *my lady*, though, Martha,' he said.

'Yes, I am, aren't I?' she said with a rueful shrug. 'Your mother may never forgive me.'

'Oh, she will. I can assure you she will,' he told her with the knowledge that the Dowager Lady Elderwood would get over having to be called by that version of her title as soon as she found out why this wedding had to happen so fast.

Martha wasn't quite so sure but hoped Zachary knew his mother a lot better than she did. Perhaps there was a warm and loving woman under the stiff facade and she was going to be delighted to become a doting grandmama to his child.

* * *

'At last! It feels like two decades since we were alone and free to make love again instead of two months,' Zachary murmured when Martha's new maid had finally quit the room and he could shut the rest of the world out until morning.

'You were the one who insisted we must wait until we were wed,' Martha told him with a cool look to say *And why was that, my lord?*

'Not because I don't want you, you gapeseed,' he told her as if he was thoroughly exasperated by her lack of confidence in her own allure.

'Well that's not very polite, is it? I am your wife.'

'Oh, yes, I certainly know that after today, but you had best not try me too hard, lest I want my wife and lover too hastily for comfort. I promised myself you were going to be my lady before I laid my lusty hands on you again, but I shouldn't have been so self-righteous.'

'Oh, was that why? Then you make too many promises and I wish you had told me about it. I thought you didn't want me.'

'I want you so much I'm afraid I'll hurt you, Martha, or harm our baby,' he said and his voice was so unsteady she was lost for words.

She watched him raise a shaking hand and felt him gently smooth her short hair as if it wasn't the boyish mess she thought. How did he know that she had been feeling self-conscious about it all day? Despite that insight he seemed to think he might harm her or their child, which was absurd. At least she would have to ignore her own nerves as she tried to soothe his. 'You won't, Zachary. You couldn't hurt either me or the baby. It's simply not in you.'

'But you need gentleness and I'm not sure I have enough strength of mind left to give it to you. It's been too long since the night we made our little Chilton, Martha, and I want you so much. I ached for you every day we were apart and now you're carrying my child I feel downright dangerous because I want you so desperately.'

'And to think I thought you were one of the most intelligent men I have ever met, Lord Elderwood. We could have made love whenever we had the chance to all this last week if I'd known you wanted me back. Then you wouldn't have to put so much effort into holding yourself in check now. Anyway, Grandmama says we must not be too hasty but you are a true gentleman and she is sure you will not take any unnecessary risks with either me or the baby.'

'Kind of her to say so, but I'm not sure I have her sunny confidence in my gentlemanly self-restraint after the last two months of bitter frustration.'

'Come here and prove to both of us that she is right, then, husband, because I have longed for you as well. At first I found it hard to forgive myself for doing so because I truly loved my first husband. I hope you can accept the fact that a part of me will always love him. That doesn't mean I don't want and need you, Zachary. I yearn for your touch and long to hear your husky words as you make love to me. I want your magnificent body in every way a woman can want a man and I know we matter to one another beyond even that. You have taught me to want you so much and in so many ways that I shall never stop wanting you.'

Perhaps it was as well that Martha got no further with her list of shameless desires before he really did touch her and murmur praise in her eager ears whenever he wasn't too busy kissing her. She didn't want to think what this was, it might be love, but on the other hand it might just be him being Zachary—gallantly determined to make his new wife would feel wanted and cared for, even if he didn't love her. It felt so wonderful to luxuriate in the intimacy of his love-making once again she shut that cautious thought away for later. Now she was blissfully floating on a dreamy cloud of heated desire for this handsome husband of hers and it didn't matter. She felt so wanted that she couldn't find the right words to tell him how much she needed him. He had such strong, elegant hands but they shook as he caressed her to such shivering neediness that she was hotly, sweetly on fire for more. It felt so powerful and yet so touching that such a strong man could clamp chains on his urgent need for her sake and their baby's. Feeling the fine tremor in his great body as he gentled himself was so moving that she almost cried. Only almost. She was too busy wanting him back with every fibre of her being for her tears to fall. Knowing she could do this to him as he remade loving for her made her feel so powerful and wanted that she believed she really was beautiful and desirable and unique as he whispered that she was. His kisses were hotter now, his touch so sensuous yet gentle, and he had roused her to a slow heated passion that felt beyond even her wildest dreams—and those had been very wild since they first did this together two months ago.

He pushed her flimsy nightdress off her shoulders and down with an impatient brush of delicate lace and lawn and found the hot, wet welcome at the heart of her with a groan that told her he was caught between frustration because he thought she was fragile nowadays and his rampant eagerness to slake this lovely, aching need deep inside her with the ultimate pleasure. She smiled a witchy invitation against his lips and wriggled her very sensitive nipples against his hair-roughened torso as she let out a moan of her own to demand more. He lowered her so gently onto the bed and then entered her with such fierce chains on his inner Viking that she felt sorry for the man. Her inner muscles convulsed around him to let him know that she wouldn't break if he surged deeper and showed her what ecstasy felt like once again, but this time with added tenderness for the very small life they had made between them last time.

It felt so wonderful she let him know it with another pleasured moan and a long hum of delicious encouragement for more. It felt so right to have him inside her and within their very private marriage bed. She was awed by her eager and powerful lover and right now he unquestionably wanted her every bit as urgently as she wanted him. She took the initiative and began to move in a long, slow rhythm that soon built such a fire inside her that she heard her own cries of encouragement for him to join her climb to ecstasy. She was fleetingly surprised that she was capable of saying anything at all as the ultimate pleasure beckoned. She could tell he was so close to it as well and he had to be straining every nerve and instinct to hold himself back so that she could get to her climax before he did, and bless the darling man for being her perfect lover.

His skin tasted salty with the effort of fighting his driving need for satisfaction. She marvelled that he had ever doubted he would be able to gentle himself for her when he was such a strong man in every sense of that word. She smoothed his tense back with admiring hands. His mighty muscles and tempered strength felt blissfully familiar as she purred with delight while he rose and fell almost imperceptibly to give her time and the restraint she was beyond even wanting now. He kept the weight of his body firmly on his arms so none of it rested on hers, and she praised his straining muscles under satin skin, then the rough masculine hair on his forearms as she keened for more, for the heady, yearning conclusion they were heading for so relentlessly but so frustratingly slowly because he cared about her pleasure ahead of his own.

Tears formed in her eyes and she kissed his straining shoulders when their ride went deeper and faster and, to her infinite satisfaction, she felt the first ripples of her climax tighten on his mighty male member as ecstasy shot through her. She cried out his name in the extremes of pleasure. Flew headlong into the complete togetherness of lovers; forgot where one began and the other started; tumbled into joy with his arms so strong above her and him shouting out her name as they came together again at last. Her head went back in a final convulsion of soaring pleasure, although she could still sense him worrying about her as she drifted back to earth and she whispered reassurances that nothing they had just done together could hurt her or their unborn child.

'It's all right, my darling,' she whispered huskily, and without even realising she had given so much away. 'We are both safe and I know we always will be with you to care so much about us. You are a good man, Zachary. Right now you feel so very good inside me I want to do it all again as soon as we have got our breath back. You really have missed me, haven't you, my lord?'

'Only like the sun during an arctic winter, or everything in life that makes it seem worth living,' he growled as if he had rasped his voice raw keeping himself in check.

She wondered if he had felt her heart leap before he stretched away from her to rest his weight on his extended arms and withdraw from her sated, pleasured body as he thought a considerate husband should. It was such a pleasure to hear him say those wonderful words, but she didn't quite believe him. She still smiled secretively, smugly, as she lay prone and pleasured and almost exhausted in their marriage bed. She felt him flop down beside her as if it had cost him even more than she knew to be her gentled lover on their wedding night. Maybe it was just as well that all the candles on the nightstand had gone out so he couldn't see that she was both smiling and silently crying with the dazed pleasure of it all and the loneliness of being separate from him again.

The loneliness inside her was asking if those were the sort of gallant words a finely educated and deeply sensitive viscount told his lovers as well as his wife. The glow of pleasure still wondrous inside her wanted to believe she was special to him, that she was the only one who ever brought out the poetry in him. Truth be told, he was a fine man who would always want the woman bearing his children to feel cherished and special. And she did; she felt pampered and very wanted as she heard his breathing calm and deepen. She still felt a twist of forbidden longing for the frantic coupling he had tried so hard not to give her. She wanted everything they could be together, but of course she couldn't ask him for it because they really did need to consider their child. So she lay there wishing instead that she had thought to ask her grandmother when a baby usually quickened. Maybe when it did she would know what made it happy and what didn't and maybe wild heat would not seem so impossible as it did right now when her baby felt small and fragile inside her.

Martha Chilton lay beside her husband and felt him drifting off to sleep. It felt so intimate and precious but her doubts came crowding back in to stop her falling into a rosy dream as she lay next to him.

Could she let herself believe he would really have come to find her after going to Holdfast last week? Knowing him, he would have felt he had to say he had meant to do so all along and he had always wanted to marry her. It must have been a kind lie. She had to protect herself and her child from the fantasy Zachary loved as well as wanted her. If she wasn't careful, she would convince herself he must love her to make such sweet, hot love to her that her body was still singing with little shocks of remembered pleasure.

She felt so cherished right now that it would be so easy to deceive herself that she was special to him and always would be. She had been a naval lieutenant's widow, and the granddaughter of a not particularly well off Lakeland squire whose noble connections were far in the past. The honourable Zachary Chilton would protect and cherish the mother of his child but would he ever love her? Probably not, she decided with a sigh, then went to sleep because it seemed easier than lying next to him and dreaming impossible things.

Chapter Fifteen

A month after their wedding, Martha got to the end of her letter and blurted out the feelings she had been fighting all that time. 'I can't stay here,' she said at last and saw stark shock on Zachary's face before he blanked it out. His ice blue eyes went so cold and guarded that she barely recognised him as her husband. 'No, not that,' she said as he clearly thought she meant forever. 'I don't mean never.'

'What *do* you mean, then?' he said gruffly.

'Grandfather needs me. I have to go back to Greygil and help him run the farms before he kills himself,' she said, waving her grandmother's letter to explain it must be urgent or Grandmama would not have mentioned it.

Luckily her morning sickness had subsided at last so she could join him at the breakfast table before he was busy with his day and before her mother-in-law was up and about. Martha was heartily bored for most of the day now she wasn't feeling like a delicate hothouse flower every morning, and the thought of being needed at Greygil felt very attractive despite the sobering fact that Zachary would not be there.

'You are not racing about the fells and lakes doing heaven knows how much harm to yourself and the baby, Martha. I won't have it.'

Hadn't he noticed she had red hair, the true colour of it visible now as her short hair grew and the last bits of darkness were gradually cut away? She counted to ten and smoothed the mop that was determined to curl, and reminded herself it would be bad for the baby if she lost her temper. *'You won't have it?'* she echoed flatly, feeling Tolbourne's control of her sister's life sitting between them like a threat.

'Don't,' he said, as if it had occurred to him as well and he hated it. 'I can't let you keep forgetting you are carrying our child and risk too much, Martha. Please don't tell me you wouldn't because I know you. In the heat of the moment you will do what needs doing then worry yourself sick about it later.'

He was right and she wanted to be furious with him for knowing her so well, but she stared warily back at him instead, unwilling to admit she longed to have her old active life back, only with him in it to add comfort and joy. She was so used to being busy that she hated being idle and decorative and bored at beautiful, intimidating Flaxonby Hall. She dressed finely, moved carefully and tried hard to learn the endless lessons her mother-in-law was trying to teach her. Lady Elderwood was doing her best to make her daughter-in-law understand the complexities of running this great house and the importance of being dignified and composed and gracious to all and sundry. The trouble was, Martha didn't feel like a great lady and she wasn't being dignified or composed or even very gracious about it.

'I can't simply abandon them, Zachary. Perhaps I could train up a manager for them or find good tenants for the Home Farm, but you must understand that I need to do something. It sounds as if Grandfather is doing far too much now I am not there to do it for him. Grandmama is terrified he will have an accident out on the fells or strain his heart or whatever other terrors she must have been brooding over to pour it all out to me when she has been trying so hard not to worry me.'

'Your apple didn't fall far from his tree, did it?' he said. It made her smile and she didn't want to, drat the man.

'I suppose not,' she agreed and smiled reluctantly. 'But I'm so bored here, Zachary,' she admitted at last with a gusty sigh. 'Your housekeeper doesn't need any directions for running your house. Cook could prepare a banquet at an hour's notice without me. Even the gardeners know what to send up to the house without me having to ask them and I think the flowers must arrange themselves behind.'

'Poor little viscountess,' he joked, but it hit hard.

'I'm just not any good at it, Zachary. You should have married my sister.'

'What an appalling idea,' he replied, shaking his head and looking as if it really was. 'I pity her former lot in life, respect her for not even trying to pass off her lover's child as mine, but she was never the Tolbourne sister I wanted. I only want the one who came downstairs dressed in Lady Fetherall's ridiculously revealing clothes the first night we met, the one I could hardly wait to get out of them and into the marriage bed, the one I married a whole glorious month ago.'

'I know,' she said with a smile at the memory of their first lovemaking and many more since their wedding night.

'But you still are not going to Greygil alone. You can't be trusted.'

'You don't trust me?'

'No. You'll forget about the baby and jump into action whenever a ewe needs lambing or a cow has to be helped to calve.'

'Oh, that sort of *don't trust me*,' she said unwarily.

'Do you think I don't know *you* because I once mistook you for your sister?'

'I deceived you, though, didn't I?' she persisted for some stupid reason. 'I have trapped you.'

'What an honourable fool you do think me.'

'No, but I think you lost too much when I agreed to impersonate my sister. You had to break your promise to your grandmother and your father and forget about your duty to poor old Holdfast Castle because of me and now you have lost your freedom as well.'

'No, that's ridiculous, Martha. You saved me from a cynical arranged marriage. You have remade me, and I like this life much better than the one I had prepared myself to endure with your half-sister. And in the end, Holdfast is only a pile of stones. Now I'm free of the shadows *my* grandfather cast, I can spend the rest of my life enjoying being with you and our children since I'm not bound to the past like a prisoner any longer. Of course I want our child, you idiot, but I wanted you first—so much that it truly didn't matter to me whether we had one or not. I already love our child, before you start doubting that as well, but you are my wife, Martha. My lady. Don't even think of going to Greygil without me because I don't intend to be parted from you ever again.'

'It might take some time to find Grandfather a good manager and finally get him to agree to let the Home Farm,' she said. Zachary had said so much despite not actually speaking the words she longed to hear. She knew she was a very lucky woman. They were so much happier than most aristocratic couples, and she would be a fool to argue that wanting wasn't the same as loving.

'I might have found one already,' he said.

'Who is he, then?'

'Me,' he said, pretending to be modest and failing rather badly.

'But you're a viscount, not a farmer or a land agent.'

'I'm all three, if you will only realise that's what I do all day when I'm not too busy loving you or holding you while you're being horribly sick because you're carrying my child. You will have to teach me the quirks of farming in your part of the country but that gives me an excuse to spend nearly every moment of the day with you while I'm learning.'

'But you're needed here, Zachary. You must be.'

'It's high time Max stopped idling about at Cambridge and learned to manage an estate. He can come home and find out what a hard day's work feels like while I concentrate on Greygil and on you.'

'You truly mean to do this, then?'

'Of course I do. It's the ideal solution for now. Once we have found out what your grandfather wants to do about his farms in the long run, we can plan for it as soon as the baby is safely born.'

'I suspect what he really wants is for me to stay there and bring up his great-grandchild at Greygil.'

'In time maybe we can share him or her between Greygil and here, so we can keep my land agent and my mother happy as well as your grandparents. Mama is longing to meet and spoil her latest grandchild.'

Martha liked the sound of living part of the year at Greygil with Zachary and teaching their children both sides of their heritage. She was a lot less sure the Dowager Lady Elderwood was going to be a doting grandmother to her child, but so many unlikely things had happened this year that she supposed even that wonder was possible.

'Isn't it the most beautiful sight you ever saw, Zachary?'

'Indeed it is,' he replied and Martha turned her gaze from the fine view of her beloved Cumberland fells and lakes in the early-June sunshine to look at him. He was a true Yorkshireman; his ready agreement to her question didn't sound quite right. '*You* are,' he told her so softly that her heart raced. She badly wanted to believe he meant it.

'With this wild boyish haircut and freckles, and that's before we even mention how fat I'm getting.'

'With your glorious red hair finally free of false colour and your golden kissable freckles…and it's not fat; it's my baby,' he said. His voice had gone gravelly with something hot and promising it was best she didn't think about when they were all the way out here.

She didn't doubt he loved the fact that their child was now openly showing on her body at five months and, as this playful summer breeze was plastering her much-washed cambric gown against her body it was even more obvious than usual.

'You are the most beautiful sight I ever saw, Martha, and you just get lovelier with each day that passes.'

'My sister has always been the beauty of the family.'

'No, your sister might have the same lovely features as you do,' he said, tracing her russet brows with a shiveringly light touch that set her heart racing. Watching her breathe light and fast between parted lips, he ran his finger gently down her pert nose, gave her full and aching lips a quick, fond brush as if he dared not linger there because he knew he would get distracted, then he gently raised her chin with it so she had to meet his eyes and let him see what he had done to her this time. 'She lacks your fiery spirit and total loyalty to those you love, my Martha. From a distance or in the dark your sister might look like you, but she is nothing like you on the inside. I want you so much I can't understand why you still don't believe me.'

He sounded frustrated and sincere. She knew he really did want her as much as he said he did after three whole months of wedded bliss. She wanted him very much too, but they were miles from home and she was supposed to be showing him something up on the fell that she had forgotten about in the heat of the moment. Best try to remember what it was, then, although he had stirred up a storm of passion that made her want to be shockingly reckless with him and never mind where they were.

'You are my lion-hearted wife and I only want you, Martha,' Zachary said, as if he found it deeply frustrating that they could not indulge their passion for one another here and now. She hardly dared believe he truly thought she was more attractive than her famously beautiful sister.

'And I want you too, Zachary,' she told him truthfully. That was one of the advantages of being married to an attentive and dedicated lover—she could be honest about how much she wanted him. 'I want you too much and I wish that we were closer to home so we could do something about it.'

'You know this place like the back of your hand. Can't you think of somewhere private between here and there?' he asked with a glint in his eyes that argued there must be some sort of hidden refuge for them in all his wide acres.

'Oh, dear, what *have* I done to you, Lord Elderwood?' she said with a witchy smile, but she racked her brains for that trysting place, since she didn't want to wait until they were home either.

'Better ask yourself what I have done to *you*, my lady,' he said with a wicked, predatory smile and a possessive hand on her swollen belly to say exactly what that was and how very much he liked it.

'You are a wicked man, my lord, going about the countryside seducing respectable countrywomen like me.'

'Only the one, only you' he argued softly, and kissed her so urgently she decided a secluded hollow nearby had enough stunted thorn trees growing around it to hide his latest seduction of this very willing countrywoman from any prying eyes that might be passing.

Lying in his arms some considerable time later, she felt deliciously languid and pleased with herself, and delighted he was looking much the same. She grasped his nearest hand to place it on her bump. 'Feel,' she said urgently. 'Can you feel him moving this time?'

'Him?' he said with raised eyebrows and an indulgent smile as he splayed his long-fingered hand over her hastily bared stomach and tried to catch the flutter of movement she was still so awed to feel now their baby had quickened.

'Well, it seems wrong to call the little mite an it. Maybe we can say he and she on alternate days, but will you mind very much if she's a girl, Zachary?' Even with her lover lazily smoothing her rounding belly and his strong body curled around her so protectively and possessively, she held her breath as she waited for his answer.

'Mind? Why should I mind? I'll be delighted if she's a girl. She might have your glorious hair and dark green eyes. Although, come to think about it, that would mean most of the males in the north country beating a path to our door long before I'm ready to send her suitors to the right about.'

'I suspect she would kill her own dragons and choose her own knight, whatever we had to say about it. Perhaps she will have your lion's mane and eyes of silver blue, which will only make those suitors buzz round us like bees to honey all the sooner.'

'Or maybe she will go her own way and choose bits of both of us and the rest of our families. I wish I could feel her moving as well but as she's inside you I suppose it's probably only right you two to get acquainted first.'

'I suspect he's going to be as restless as his papa when he gets bigger and is impatient to get out into the world. Then you will certainly be able to see and feel him moving, according to my grandmother. And don't forget he's a boy today, Zachary. You can be overprotective about our daughter tomorrow.'

'If I don't get one of those this time, we'll just have to keep trying.' he countered with a smug look, but as she could never imagine finding this part of their marriage a duty. that seemed excusable.

'A viscount does need an heir, though, doesn't he?' she said wistfully.

'This one doesn't care if you have daughters by the dozen, my lady, as long as they are all born healthy and you are safe and well.'

'I think a dozen might be excessive, my lord,' she murmured with a sleepy smile and decided nothing was urgent enough to worry about outside this hidden hollow just now. She let his now almost soothing touch mesmerise her into lying here in the dappled shade of the ancient thorn trees and letting go of her worries. She almost let the word *love* slip out of her sleepy mouth as she nestled even further into the familiar comfort of his body, but even as she tumbled into sleep in his arms, she managed not to murmur a word she knew he would not want to hear.

Chapter Sixteen

Martha almost forgot to worry about Zachary being a nobleman while he was busy learning to run her grandfather's farms. He didn't seem to worry about his rank and responsibilities while he was here so she did her best not to either. She loved being able to walk and talk with him all day, to share her thoughts and knowledge and hear his in return.

She already knew he had been forced to grow up too soon when his father died, but as she heard his tales of his younger brother and sisters' exploits and misadventures, she realised he must have felt too responsible for them to be the carefree boy he should have been. He had done his best for all three of his siblings and tried to be a substitute father to them, although he had still been a boy himself.

Her love for this almost too strong man was becoming hard to keep pent up inside her. Sometimes she physically ached to tell him how she really felt, but what if it spoiled everything they had managed to build together since were married? He had already had too many burdens placed on his shoulders after being left with his title and such a large estate. Was it really fair to add her unrequited love to the load? No, it wasn't, so she would just have to keep silent and hope he wanted her child enough to stay here even when she became so big he no longer wanted to lie with her.

Her heart might break if he ever turned wanting, seducing silver-blue eyes on another woman, but for now she had everything she wanted right here, beside her, with her, enjoying her. So she would keep on enjoying it and enjoying him. Even if it wasn't forever, it was very good for now. After all, she was his wife and the only woman who could bear him legitimate children. Yet such practical resolutions were easy enough to make but so very hard to keep.

Her decision not to risk telling him what he meant to her felt lonely and a little bit weak as she sat sewing very badly one morning while he read his letters. It was raining outside after days of beautiful June sun and all the chances that made for snatched summer loving were being washed away. Snug here in their private sitting room, she didn't want to brave the rain for once. She felt so lazily content listening to it falling from the security of their cosy room she wanted to stay here with Zachary all day and be deliciously idle for once.

Not that he was very good at doing nothing. Soon he would get restless and want to be busy again, despite the rain, but she was feeling languid and content to be with him today and never mind work for once. Some days she hardly recognised the busy and determined woman she had been before she met Viscount Elderwood that fateful night in Kent. She was forever falling asleep at unexpected moments or feeling driven to learn all sorts of things she had never been interested in before—like sewing, for example. She was trying to make a baby smock—but it was not very good.

Meanwhile, Zachary read out bits out of Max's latest letter, and his little brother's wry comments on his own lessons in estate management made her laugh. She tried to sew a straight seam in the tiny garment she already suspected no baby would ever be the right shape to fit into, and it wasn't until Zachary swore and threw his next letter down in disgust that she noticed how completely his mood had changed.

'What's the matter?' she said, throwing her lumpy needlework aside with a sigh of relief.

'Damn him,' he muttered distractedly, and his frown reminded her of the icy Viking lord she had first met at Tolbourne House. She shivered with apprehension, feeling as if an ill wind was about to blast her shiny new world apart and she hadn't even sensed it coming. 'Read it,' he said abruptly, and began to pace the room as if he couldn't contain his feelings any other way.

'Oh, Tolbourne,' she said with a grimace when she saw the signature and dropped it like a hot coal.

'You still need to read what he says.'

'Why? He wrote to you, not me,' she said, holding the letter at arm's length as if it might burn her. It did feel dangerous. She should have known the devious old man would not leave them alone now she had wed a viscount.

'Of course he did. His granddaughters were only ever the means to an end as far as he was concerned,' Zachary said tersely but waved his hand at the letter she held as if she still needed to read it.

'True,' she said and tried to concentrate on the words in front of her although she didn't want to know what Tolbourne thought or said after what he had done to Caro. 'He wants to *give* you Holdfast?' she exclaimed.

She was horrified but didn't want Zachary to know that Tolbourne still had the power to hurt her. Or why the idea of him accepting the place felt like being faced with a dangerous cliff edge. She felt dizzy at the chasm Tolbourne seemed to have created between her and Zachary with that one carefully placed charge dropped into their placidly domestic morning.

Of course Tolbourne would not send her news of this backhanded offer of Holdfast. As far as he was concerned, she didn't matter, but Zachary had longed to get hold of the place since he was a boy. Maybe he would be too blinded by the idea of getting it at no cost and he wouldn't even notice that the old man's olive branches had poisoned thorns.

'Why?' she said at last, unable to look at the letter again and see for herself.

'Because his great-grandson will be able to inherit it one day and the whole world will know that our son owes Holdfast Castle to his great-grandfather.'

'Is that what he says?'

'Of course not, but he is only offering it to me because one of his granddaughters did what he wanted and married a viscount, even if you are the one he cast out as a child.'

'The one he disowned and exposed to public scandal.'

'And by doing so he made you the lucky one. You came here to be loved by your maternal grandparents instead of bullied and used by him.'

Zachary carried on pacing as if his thoughts were so full of plans for Holdfast that he had hardly noticed she didn't want Tolbourne to have a toehold in their lives. It didn't feel right that her wicked grandfather would be able to boast that his great-grandson would inherit an ancient name and title from his father one day, but would owe Holdfast to his paternal great-grandfather, the son of a pauper who had made a vast fortune.

Martha shuddered, Tolbourne's destructive hand would blight all their lives if they let it. Zachary had wanted Holdfast badly enough to agree to marry her sister for it, so of course he would leap at the offer of it for nothing more than it had already cost him. Except Tolbourne thought everything on earth had its price and he was trying to buy their baby's future.

'I could so easily have been consigned to the poorhouse when he rejected me,' she argued. She didn't want Zachary to know how much she dreaded him accepting Tolbourne's so-called gift. She dreaded him being bitter about it when possession of Holdfast ate into his fortune and tore apart their compromise between Greygil and Flaxonby.

'If he had kept you with him your life would have been a constant battle, Martha,' Zachary argued. 'You would have fought him tooth and nail on your sister's behalf and it would have broken you.'

Zachary understood her almost too well. At least he didn't add *and you were only a girl*, but she felt those words hang in the air. It was what the old man was really so furious about when he sent her packing—he had been saddled with two grand-daughters and no boy to take his grand ambitions into the future and inherit his name.

She *would* have fought Tolbourne every step of the way for Caro's sake. Zachary's understanding of her character should warm her, but she was too aware of what he'd had to kiss goodbye to when Caro had wed another man to feel anything but cold. Zachary had had to break his solemn promise to his father and grandmother because of what she and Caro had done. It was a fault in the fabric of their marriage that could unravel it if Tolbourne was allowed to seize control of her life instead of Caro's.

'My sister would have had an easier time if I had been there to encourage her,' she said, as if her sister was at the heart of her worries. But she wasn't this time. Her husband and unborn child were at the centre of her world now, but she wasn't sure she and the baby were the centre of his. Holdfast was tantalisingly within his reach. His old promise to get it back was luring him in so strongly he probably didn't even realise the danger.

'Tolbourne would have punished every defiant word and used you as a stick to beat your sister into obedience.'

They were having a conversation about a childhood that had never existed, while Tolbourne's letter lay like a serpent on the table between them.

'Maybe,' she admitted reluctantly and felt like a coward for letting him have this conversation instead of the one they ought to be having.

She didn't want Zachary to know about the stupid soreness in her heart. He was about to get what he had always wanted but she had so badly wanted them to be free of past. There were too many oaths sworn at too high a cost. Such unhappiness and grief had been caused by his family's quest to get the poor old place back. Yet she could see how strongly he must be tempted. He had thought Holdfast was lost to his family forever, but now it was being offered to him on a silver salver.

'I dare say he has already tried to sell the place since he disowned your sister as well as you, but he must have found out that nobody else wants it in the state he let it get into,' Zachary said with a rueful smile when he finally stopped pacing, but her mouth felt too frozen to return it.

'But *you* do,' she said, and he took too long to shrug, as if he wished the place didn't matter but it did.

'It is a sad travesty of its former self,' he said. He clearly wanted to rescue the place for its own sake, and somehow that made things worse.

'True,' she said numbly.

Zachary seemed so wrapped up in the novelty of finally getting what he wanted at last that he didn't even notice she wasn't as keen on the idea as he was.

'Gone? What do you mean she's gone? She can't have.'

Zach watched his grandfather-in-law's austere face for the smile he had learned to look for in the older man's still very acute grey eyes but there wasn't even a hint it now. Squire Winton looked sternly back at the man he had almost seemed resigned to his precious granddaughter marrying until now.

'Nevertheless, she has done so, but she has left you this,' the Squire Winton said with a spark of pity in his eyes this time.

Zach's heart thundered in his ears as he eyed the single folded sheet of paper as if it might bite him. 'But she's with child. She shouldn't be travelling on her own,' he protested.

'Try telling her that. She's with child, lad, not ill. Healthy as a fell pony, my Martha is, and twice as stubborn. Still, I don't suppose she'll break from travelling a few miles in that fancy carriage of yours you would insist on keeping here.'

'Where's she gone, then?'

'Try reading her letter. Maybe it will tell you.'

Zach broke the seal impatiently and quickly scanned the lines she had left for her very concerned husband to read after she was gone. Why the devil did she need to go and see the former Lady Fetherall when she must be so near her time that Caroline would not want visitors? He began to pace restlessly and didn't even notice that Martha's grandfather had left the room so Zach could stamp about and curse in peace. He read on and only just stopped himself closing his fist on the first letter he had ever received from his own wife.

Martha had turned his whole life upside down from the moment he set eyes on her and he liked it so much better this way up. But it hurt him to know that his wife valued her sister's views about their grandfather's offer so much that she had set out for Harrogate when she was with child herself. She should have stayed here, with him, until she was safely delivered. He read through her scanty message again and frowned at his own need to be her everything, and never mind Mrs Harmsley.

Zach wanted to be his wife's wisest counsellor, her rock and her other half. She sounded as if he was none of those things in the brusque missive she had left to be given to him when she was already well on her way. Zach had been too far up on the fells today to have had even the slightest notion of what was going on behind his back and she had seized her chance to bolt when he wasn't around to stop her.

He shivered as he tried to force his way through this storm of contrary emotions and the desolation of missing Martha, as if a crucial part of him had been cut away. If this was what he got for trying to woo her without words, then he was going to let them all out next time they were both in the same place. If she didn't want his love as well as his abiding passion, well, that was just too bad, because she had it anyway and he wasn't going to keep quiet about it any longer.

Dear Zachary...

That was how her confounded letter began. Not quite a formal greeting but nowhere near as wifely as he would have liked. He wanted her to write *'Dearest Zachary,'* or *'My Dearest Love'* but they were clearly pipe dreams and *'Dear Zachary'* was all the intimacy she was prepared to allow him. Her refusal to say more squeezed his heart like a cold hand. Was that the best he was ever going to get from his stubborn, infuriating, enchanting and beloved Lady Elderwood? No, he refused to kill off all hope of more ever growing between them. He would tell her he loved her and she would just have to live with it. Maybe it would make her think about what lay beneath her insatiable passion for him as a lover and he would find out if she could ever feel more than *'Dear Zachary'* for him. And she carried on as if he were a nodding acquaintance.

I need to consult my sister about the offer Tolbourne has made you. Caro was his only acceptable heiress and grandchild for twenty years, until she crossed him and he disinherited her. She deserves to know what is being proposed and I am quite sure he will not have told her. I believe she also needs to know how Tolbourne forced you into the engagement just as he forced her.

I will think very hard about his offer whilst I am away. Your honour and pride will tell you to seize it and keep your promises to your father and grandmother at last, but trust me when I say Tolbourne is not a man to give away something for nothing.

I beg you to hold back from replying to his letter until my return, although maybe you should tell your family about it and they will remind you what burdens restoring such a ruinous old place will place on you. It would take many years to get it back into any sort of order, so they probably deserve to know what is being proposed since Flaxonby will have to pay for much of that restoration until the Holdfast estate can cover its own costs again.

Please ask them not to discuss it with anyone else until the matter is settled and don't concern yourself about me. I am as robust as ever now and must see my sister before she is brought to bed and I am too big to travel.

I will take the greatest care of our child, my lord, so please do not fret about us while I am away. Look after yourself and please stay here and make sure Grandfather does not tramp the fells all day while I am gone.

It ended with *'Yours ever, Martha Chilton,'* as if he were a distant relative rather than her frustrated husband. Zach paced even faster as he argued with his absent wife as though she were only hiding in a corner.

'You know very well you have tied my hands behind my back with that last duty, you exasperating woman. I can't follow you, can I? I'm only here to stop your grandfather wearing himself out managing the farm on his own, and he would do exactly that if Thor and I were to gallop after you. And why is your sister's opinion gold and silver and mine no good at all?'

Zach paused his pacing for a moment and thought harder about the last bit. He didn't want Martha to value Mrs Harmsley's opinion more than his—he wanted *all* her confidence and trust. He couldn't spare any for the scared little mouse who had caused this mess. That wasn't right, though, was it? Temper—and a large slice of hurt—were making him unjust. It wasn't even a mess really, and Lady Fetherall's dilemma and subsequent decision had changed the whole course of his life for the better. Martha *was* his life now—she was his everything, all that truly mattered in one stubborn and adorable feminine package. Caroline Harmsley was a scared woman who had nearly had her spirit broken by her own grandfather but she had caused Zach to meet and marry the one woman he truly wanted, admired, and trusted.

So it wasn't a mess at all. He should be eternally grateful to Mrs Harmsley instead of cursing her for being the person Martha wanted to consult instead of him. He should have thought more deeply about his wife's feelings when he had read Tolbourne's letter and been so tempted by the carrot being dangled in front of him.

Martha's unwritten reproach for seeing only what he wanted to in Tolbourne's unexpected letter stung because it was justified. Of course she hated the idea of taking anything from the mean old man who had cruelly cast her aside as a child and who was trying to control her life again after all these years of cold neglect. Zach should have stepped back far enough to see what a stupid idea it was before she went. How could he even think of putting himself in the old tyrant's debt like that? How could he ignore what Tolbourne had done to both of his granddaughters in his hard-hearted quest for a title for his great-grandson?

Zach had already accepted that Holdfast was a lost cause when he married Martha, yet he had leaped at Tolbourne's bait like an eager fool and forgot to look past it. That is, until he had taken a long walk up the fells to the most remote part of the Home Farm and sanity had finally crept back in. Would that it had done so before Martha had decided to look for advice elsewhere. Now he had to contain his frustration and fear and hopes of being forgiven for being such an idiot until his wife decided to come home again.

Chapter Seventeen

It was a good job Caro and Harmsley were settled in his comfortable house near Harrogate until their baby was born because Martha couldn't wait to get home. Even the next village would have felt too far away from her husband. It had been wonderful to see her little sister feeling so contented in her marriage and both of them longing to meet her baby in a matter of days. Mr Harmsley clearly doted on his wife, although Martha was glad Zachary didn't fuss over her as much as Caro's husband did over her, but Caro seemed to like it. Despite her love for her half-sister and her relief that Caro was happy, they had not been allowed enough time together in their formative years to live under the same roof in perfect ease and comfort.

Martha belonged with Zachary now; he was her family and every moment she spent away from him had felt wrong. It had felt wrong from the moment his fine carriage was carrying her away from Greygil but she had a plan. If it came off, maybe he could still keep his promises and yet not allow Tolbourne his unjust triumph.

Now she was nearly home at last and she held her breath as she waited for her first sight of her beloved home with her beloved husband inside it—or at least she hoped he was. If he was out on the fells, or maybe even so furious with her that he had gone back to Flaxonby in disgust, then it would serve her right for disappearing when his back was turned. But she desperately hoped that he was waiting for her here because she was longing to see him again.

He would be here, her wiser self—the one who wasn't panicking—stepped in to reassure her. He wouldn't leave Grandfather struggling alone and even Zachary couldn't supervise the haymaking in the rain. It pleased her to know that every other female in the area was being denied the chance to see him bare chested and magnificent for a little longer. Good, maybe she would sew him into his shirts every morning to make sure they never got a glimpse of her magnificent husband naked from the waist up.

Then the carriage was drawing up in the stable yard at last and Martha had to impatiently wait for the steps to be lowered. She wanted to jump down and find out if he was here or not straight away, but she must put the welfare of their baby before her need to see its father again after a whole night away. There was a flurry of greetings and fussing, and even the baby was restless if the cartwheels it seemed to be turning inside her were anything to go by.

'Where's Zachary?' she demanded as soon as she could get a word in edgeways.

'Here,' his deep voice informed her from just inside the back door, and everyone else could have been talking Greek for all she understood as she stared hungrily at him and he stared moodily back. 'Where the devil have you been?' he demanded abruptly.

'I told you, I have been to see my sister.'

'For two whole days? She's only living in Harrogate for goodness' sake.'

'And you would be the first person to tell me I hadn't taken enough care of our child if I raced there and back as fast as your horses would go.'

'Aye,' he said, running a distracted hand through his tawny locks and making her long to either smooth them down again or make them even wilder while she persuaded him to forget that she had gone away without telling him. 'I would,' he said and gave her an even more complicated look that said he wasn't sure if he wanted to shake her or make love to her.

'Come into our parlour,' she said with a hasty look around and discovered everyone else had tactfully left them to argue this out. Maybe he had been stamping about like a bear with a sore paw while she was gone. It was wrong for that idea to make her feel so much better.

'In all my dirt?' he argued. 'Your grandmother would skin me.'

'Does it look as if she cares, my lord?' she said with a gesture at the empty entrance hall and so many closed doors along the corridors she could practically feel everyone waiting for the explosion he looked as if he had been working up to ever since she sneaked off to see Caro without him.

'Maybe not, but *I* still do.'

'You would,' she said, disappointed that he cared more about getting rid of his dirt than greeting his prodigal wife properly and in private.

'Stay here while I change my boots and wash,' he demanded tightly. Maybe he did care about her a little since he wasn't actually shouting yet.

She marched to their private sitting room and sat there like the quiet and obedient wife they both knew by now she was never going to be, but which she was being one today only because of the baby. It felt as if Zachary was punishing her for going away by withholding even a smile to say he was glad she was back again, but she wasn't like Caro; she couldn't sit still and meekly await her fate.

She got to her feet and paced while she waited for him. She caught a glimpse of herself in the mirror over the mantelpiece and decided it was a good thing she had stopped at an inn half an hour ago to refresh herself and at least try to look her best for her reunion with her husband. Six months on from that never-to-be-forgotten first night with Zachary, at least her hair was all her own colour now and just about long enough to be wound into a cunning knot of curls that almost hid the fact they were so short.

She was beginning to see why women were said to be 'big with child' and raised her gaze from her swollen belly to meet her own eyes in the mirror. They were dark with apprehension and a pinch of wild hope that Zachary might love her a little bit after all to be so grumpy at her for going away so suddenly. She watched her mouth tremble at the idea that the next few minutes could be crucial to the rest of her life, but she didn't have enough time to work herself into a defensive temper before he strode in and shut the door smartly behind him. At least he had hurried over his washing and not even stopped to put on new boots or tuck his clean shirt into his breeches. She loved him even more when he was dishevelled and hasty than when he was every inch a lord and about as elegant as a man could get.

'Why, Martha?' he demanded as if he couldn't wait a moment longer to demand a good reason for her hasty journey.

'I had to tell Caro that Tolbourne had offered you Holdfast.'

'Why? She's your sister, not the oracle at Delphi.'

'He used Holdfast to force you to marry her and she needed to know.'

'You said that before, but I still don't know why.'

'I couldn't let her go on thinking you were greedy for Tolbourne's money or that you were being blackmailed into marrying her over some disgraceful family secret,' she admitted. She didn't know why her journey had felt quite so urgent herself until she got there. When she did get to Harrogate, she'd realised she had to convince Caro and her new husband that Zachary was a good man with a perfectly honourable weak spot that Tolbourne had exploited to make him agree to marry Caro.

'But I was,' Zachary said bleakly and refused to look at her.

'Not the way she thought.'

'I don't much care what she thinks; she isn't you, Martha. You're the only Tolbourne sister I really care about. I like your sister now more than I ever thought I could when I asked her to marry me, but she has a husband to worry about her; she doesn't need me.'

'I still had to tell her.'

'No, you didn't. You could have written to her. None of it is disgraceful except for Tolbourne's part in it. The whole world can know about my part in the fiasco of an engagement to the wrong sister. I don't care what the *ton* thinks of us either, before you start worrying about them as well.'

'You don't have to care; you were born into it,' she said with a shrug to pretend it didn't matter if she wasn't part of the same exclusive circle as he was.

'You're Squire Winton's granddaughter as well as my viscountess, Martha. Your mother must have loved your father, despite his Tolbourne blood, to have run away with him, so why do you take that fat rogue's valuation of you before your own husband's? I keep telling you you're as good as anyone but I feel like I'm wasting my breath. You're the only woman I have ever truly wanted to marry. Please leave our baby out of things this once and tell me why you refuse to believe I honour and adore you.'

He sounded driven and desperate, as if he really

did only want her. Was adoration close enough to love that the difference didn't matter? She didn't know but she couldn't fight her own nature any longer. She couldn't keep something so big to herself, even if it changed everything between them and made him feel as if he was forever treading on eggshells with his own wife.

'Because I love you, of course!' she shouted at him as if it had been forced out of her.

'At last,' he said on a great sigh that sounded so pent-up and heartfelt she couldn't look away to hide her own emotions. Instead, she met his silver-blue gaze with so much wild hope in her own it felt painful. 'At long, long last,' he added softly.

Hope wasn't a spark now; it was a blaze threatening to flare out of control. 'Why?' she asked, her heart beating like a drum as she held her breath as she waited for his answer.

'Because I love you too, you nitwit,' he said, almost echoing her words.

She was silenced by it all the same. She gasped out a pent-up breath and still couldn't speak for the shock of hearing him say the words she had longed to hear for months. She tried to take in the wonder of it as the blaze of emotions in his eyes challenged her not to believe him. Didn't he know everything in her world had turned rosy? She felt as if a great weight had gone from her shoulders.

'I was transported somewhere strange and new the instant I saw you on the stairs that night, Martha.'

'Then why don't you come over here and tell me

more, husband?' she said in her best Lady Fetherall drawl. Something that had seemed so serious at
the time became a lover's game once he made sure
the door into their private parlour was firmly locked
against the rest of the world.

'I wonder if Celine still has the pattern for that
gown?' she murmured dreamily as she gazed at her
husband after he told her a few of the things that
gown had made him long to do to their very mutual
satisfaction.

It felt wonderful and so freeing to be able to look
at him without trying to hide how she felt about him
anymore. She stared into his ice-and-steel eyes, as
she had secretly longed to from the moment they
first met hers on those stairs and everything but Lord
Elderwood had faded into nothingness for an ex-
hilarating moment before reality had dashed back
in and forbade it.

'It was spectacular, but you wouldn't be able to
get into it now,' he pointed out with a fascinated caress over her swollen belly.

'Brute,' she accused him breathily, because he
seemed to find the rest of her quite interesting as
well. 'I really have no idea why I love you,' she told
him as severely as she could with nothing but a blissful smile on her face.

'But you still do,' he said. At last it wasn't even
a question and didn't that feel wonderful as well?

'I do, Zachary. I really and truly and quite inex-
plicably do love you and I always will, although you

can be so very arrogant and pleased with your lordly self at times.'

'I feel quite pleased with my lordly self right now,' he admitted with a boyish grin.

She had never seen him as carefree as he was as he settled her in front of him and told her he was going to nobly protect her from this rather lumpy old chaise with his body. A joyous future lay in front of them, right in front of them, and his hands rested on her pregnant belly again as they shared the unexpected wonder she had never thought to have.

'I do love, you, Zachary,' she told him dreamily, 'so very much. I don't know how I kept quiet about it for so long. I suspect I already loved you that night I knocked on your bedroom door to tell you I wasn't going to be there to marry you in the morning, and look what happened next,' she said with a rueful glance at her baby bump.

'I kept wondering why I was suddenly obsessed with the same woman I had so reluctantly proposed to a few weeks before. I thought I had run mad, and maybe I *had*, because I haven't been the same since I first laid eyes on you so defiant and wary and seductive in your sister's outrageous crimson gown. You make me blind to the rest of the world, speechless with wanting you, stupid with needing you, Martha.'

He shrugged as if he had run out of ways to say what he wanted. He shook his head and just looked at her with such honesty and heat and hope in his eyes as she wriggled round to watch his beloved face.

She felt something old and lost and lonely break inside her.

'The world still thinks I am illegitimate,' she told him.

'But we know they're wrong so what does it matter?'

'It will matter to our child,' she said, joining his protective hand on her distended belly with one of hers. 'To all of them,' she added. 'For this one's sake and any others we are blessed with, it's time to take control of what the world thinks of us, Zachary. I won't let that mean old man cast dark shadows on our children's lives like he did over both mine and Caro's.'

'Then I will find a way to make him take it back, but I'm not interested in him right now. He's not important.'

'I do hope I'm not dreaming again.'

'Have you dreamed of me, then?'

'Only every night since first we met. I can't tell you how cross it made me.'

'Hmm, we really need to explore those dreams more closely,' he said.

'Later,' she said, because however reluctant she was to let the world back in to this delicious idyll, it was still going on around them. 'You do know Tolbourne's offer of Holdfast as some sort of dowry for me was his way of trying to control us, don't you?' she said.

'Even I was capable of working out what he was up to once reality dawned and the mirage of being able to fulfil my father's dreams floated clean away,' he said grimly. 'It's lucky you have two wonderful grandparents, Martha, because we didn't do very well with some of the others, did we?'

'No, and that's partly why I had to see Caro, apart from making sure she knows what a gallant idiot you truly are. I couldn't let your wicked grandparents or mine control our lives any longer.'

'I won't accept Holdfast,' he told her starkly.

'You haven't told him so yet, I hope?'

'No, because you asked me not to and even if you did tie my hands about that and about coming after you, I suppose I shall have to forgive you for it sooner or later.'

'Generous,' she said ironically.

'I think so.'

'I want you to accept Holdfast,' she said and felt his caressing hand still. 'Wait, Zachary, listen. I have a plan, and if you agree to it we can frustrate Tolbourne and still honour your father's promise to get the place back one day.'

'Why don't I like the sound of this plan of yours?'

'You will. I only went away without you to make doubly sure Caro didn't want. I owed it to her to ask her face-to-face if she was interested in the castle so I would know if she was telling me the truth or not.'

'What did she say?'

'That she couldn't imagine why I would even think she wanted a grim northern stronghold, especially after Tolbourne had stripped it bare and left it to rot.'

'Neither do I.'

She shouldn't run a feather-light, exploring finger over his stern mouth and seduce him again. She was sure they had other things to do than make love on a lazy summer afternoon, if only she could remember what they were.

'Good. I don't either. I do want Tolbourne to gift it to you, though. No, wait, please hear me out,' she said when he had frowned and drew breath to bark out a refusal. 'Your lawyers must insist it comes to you free of all conditions and with a big enough endowment to help you set it to rights after all his years of rough treatment. I shall have to leave that bit to you and your no doubt very clever lawyers, my lord, since we married women don't even exist as far as the unjust laws of our land are concerned.'

'If only they knew,' he said grumpily.

'Now, don't be like that, lover.'

'Why do you want all that tied up and legal if you don't want it either, then? It would be so much better if we could write off the past and live our best lives together with this little one as soon as he or she is safely born. Revenge wouldn't taste very sweet if we had Tolbourne on our coattails for the rest of his life because he gave us Holdfast and will expect us to let him have his say in his great-grandson's life forever after because of it.'

'He won't, because the day it becomes legally yours, free and clear of all conditions and made viable by his endowment, we are going to hand it over to Max.'

'My brother, Max, the one who has his nose in a book most of the time, the one who told me on our wedding day that he's never going to get married. He's your grand plan?'

'Yes, and I think you could be a little more complimentary about it because I happen to think it's ingenious. Holdfast would be back in your family, as you promised your father and grandmother, and not a single drop of Tolbourne's blood will flow through the part of your family that will own it. Max can leave it to one of your sisters' children one day if he wants to, just so long and he doesn't try to pass it back to any of ours.'

'It's a neat plan, I'll give you that. Devious as well. I am almost afraid of you, Lady Elderwood. Remind me never to cross you.'

'Now why would you even think about doing so, Lord Elderwood? In my delicate condition it could be bad for me to be argued with, let alone crossed.'

'Delicate, my foot,' he replied with a wolfish grin that said he had thought her neat solution through and might forgive her hasty trip to see her sister without him in time because it really was as clever as she thought it was. 'I still love you though, so it must be incurable.'

'I can't tell you how pleased I am to hear it, my love,' she managed to say almost meekly. 'Now, about how much you love me,' she added with a suggestive wriggle. 'I am very eager to hear more.'

'Some things are better demonstrated than talked about, my lady,' he said with a lazy grin that said the door was locked and they had all afternoon to explore that idea further.

'Then what are you waiting for, my lord? I have been very busy about our business so it's time you rewarded my diligence, don't you?'

'I think you are a managing, devious—' he broke off at her *humph* of protest and ran his index finger over her pouting mouth so it turned into a *hmm* of happy encouragement '—delicious and intriguing woman and I'm so glad I got you with child so you had to marry me.'

'I thought the boot was on the other foot.'

'Our boots, our feet—what does it matter whose feet they're on?'

'It doesn't. Now kiss me again, Zachary, because I have been gone for a whole night and almost two days and I have missed you so much that I wished I could grow wings and fly back to you all the quicker.'

'Then don't go off without me ever again. You can kiss me this time because it felt like you were gone for a month to me, and you did write me that ridiculous letter to make it seem even longer,' he said.

'It was a very polite letter.'

'It was deplorably polite. *"Dear Zachary... Yours ever, Martha,"'* he quoted, 'as if I were the linen draper or someone you had once heard of but barely know.'

'Will *"Dearest, darling Zachary, my beloved and adored husband,"* do better next time?'

'No. Don't ever go away again and you won't need to write anything,' he said gruffly.

Martha chuckled at his grumpy expression. She turned in his arms and knelt up so she could lean over him and look deep into his eyes. 'I do, though,' she told him. 'I do love and adore you, my dearest, darling Zachary.' She kissed him, and they took shameless advantage of the fact that he had been so gruff and bad tempered while she was away that the rest of the household were staying tactfully out of the way.

* * * * *

If you enjoyed this story, be sure to pick up one of Elizabeth Beacon's other great reads

Lady Helena's Secret Husband
Falling for the Scandalous Lady

*And why not check out her trilogy
The Yelverton Marriages*

Marrying for Love or Money?
Unsuitable Bride for a Viscount
The Governess's Secret Longing

Get 4 FREE REWARDS!

We'll send you 2 FREE Books plus 2 FREE Mystery Gifts.

FREE
Value Over
$20

Both the **Harlequin® Historical** and **Harlequin® Romance** series feature compelling novels filled with emotion and simmering romance.

YES! Please send me 2 FREE novels from the Harlequin Historical or Harlequin Romance series and my 2 FREE gifts (gifts are worth about $10 retail). After receiving them, if I don't wish to receive any more books, I can return the shipping statement marked "cancel." If I don't cancel, I will receive 6 brand-new Harlequin Historical books every month and be billed just $6.19 each in the U.S. or $6.74 each in Canada, a savings of at least 11% off the cover price, or 4 brand-new Harlequin Romance Larger-Print books every month and be billed just $6.09 each in the U.S. or $6.24 each in Canada, a savings of at least 13% off the cover price. It's quite a bargain! Shipping and handling is just 50¢ per book in the U.S. and $1.25 per book in Canada.* I understand that accepting the 2 free books and gifts places me under no obligation to buy anything. I can always return a shipment and cancel at any time by calling the number below. The free books and gifts are mine to keep no matter what I decide.

Choose one: ☐ **Harlequin Historical**   ☐ **Harlequin Romance Larger-Print**
(246/349 HDN GRH7)   (119/319 HDN GRH7)

Name (please print)

Address   Apt. #

City   State/Province   Zip/Postal Code

Email: Please check this box ☐ if you would like to receive newsletters and promotional emails from Harlequin Enterprises ULC and its affiliates. You can unsubscribe anytime.

Mail to the **Harlequin Reader Service:**
IN U.S.A.: P.O. Box 1341, Buffalo, NY 14240-8531
IN CANADA: P.O. Box 603, Fort Erie, Ontario L2A 5X3

Want to try 2 free books from another series! Call 1-800-873-8635 or visit www.ReaderService.com.

*Terms and prices subject to change without notice. Prices do not include sales taxes, which will be charged (if applicable) based on your state or country of residence. Canadian residents will be charged applicable taxes. Offer not valid in Quebec. This offer is limited to one order per household. Books received may not be as shown. Not valid for current subscribers to the Harlequin Historical or Harlequin Romance series. All orders subject to approval. Credit or debit balances in a customer's account(s) may be offset by any other outstanding balance owed by or to the customer. Please allow 4 to 6 weeks for delivery. Offer available while quantities last.

Your Privacy—Your information is being collected by Harlequin Enterprises ULC, operating as Harlequin Reader Service. For a complete summary of the information we collect, how we use this information and to whom it is disclosed, please visit our privacy notice located at corporate.harlequin.com/privacy-notice. From time to time we may also exchange your personal information with reputable third parties. If you wish to opt out of this sharing of your personal information, please visit readerservice.com/consumerschoice or call 1-800-873-8635. **Notice to California Residents**—Under California law, you have specific rights to control and access your data. For more information on these rights and how to exercise them, visit corporate.harlequin.com/california-privacy.

HHHRLP22R3

Get 4 FREE REWARDS!

We'll send you 2 FREE Books plus 2 FREE Mystery Gifts.

FREE
Value Over
$20

Both the **Romance** and **Suspense** collections feature compelling novels written by many of today's bestselling authors.

YES! Please send me 2 FREE novels from the Essential Romance or Essential Suspense Collection and my 2 FREE gifts (gifts are worth about $10 retail). After receiving them, if I don't wish to receive any more books, I can return the shipping statement marked "cancel." If I don't cancel, I will receive 4 brand-new novels every month and be billed just $7.49 each in the U.S. or $7.74 each in Canada. That's a savings of at least 17% off the cover price. It's quite a bargain! Shipping and handling is just 50¢ per book in the U.S. and $1.25 per book in Canada.* I understand that accepting the 2 free books and gifts places me under no obligation to buy anything. I can always return a shipment and cancel at any time by calling the number below. The free books and gifts are mine to keep no matter what I decide.

Choose one: ☐ **Essential Romance**
(194/394 MDN GRHV)
☐ **Essential Suspense**
(191/391 MDN GRHV)

Name (please print)

Address   Apt. #

City   State/Province   Zip/Postal Code

Email: Please check this box ☐ if you would like to receive newsletters and promotional emails from Harlequin Enterprises ULC and its affiliates. You can unsubscribe anytime.

Mail to the **Harlequin Reader Service:**
IN U.S.A.: P.O. Box 1341, Buffalo, NY 14240-8531
IN CANADA: P.O. Box 603, Fort Erie, Ontario L2A 5X3

Want to try 2 free books from another series? Call 1-800-873-8635 or visit www.ReaderService.com.

HARLEQUIN
PLUS

Try the best multimedia subscription service for romance readers like you!

Read, Watch and Play.

Experience the easiest way to get the romance content you crave.

Start your **FREE TRIAL** at
<u>www.harlequinplus.com/freetrial</u>.